The House Next Door

Will Macmillan Jones

First edition 2016 by Red Kite Publishing Limited

www.redkitepublishing.net

Text Copyright 2015 by Will Macmillan Jones

Will Macmillan Jones asserts the moral right to be identified as the author of this work under the Copyright, Designs and Patents Act 1988.

All characters and events in this publication other than those clearly in the public domain, are fictitious and any resemblance to real persons, living or dead, is purely coincidental.

All rights reserved. No part of this publication may be reproduced, stored in or introduced into a retrieval system, or transmitted, in any form or by any means, including but not limited to electronic, mechanical, photocopying or recording, without the prior written permission of the publisher.

A CIP catalogue record for this book is available from the British Library.

Find out more about the author on
www.willmacmillanjones.com

Cover art by Hazel Butler: www.thebookshinebandit.com

All rights reserved.

ISBN:
978-1523344000

DEDICATION

Absent Friends.

Books by Will Macmillan Jones

Paranormal Mysteries

The Mister Jones Collection

The Showing	2014
Portrait of a Girl	2015
The House Next Door	2016

Childrens Books

Snort and Wobbles	2014
Return of The Goblins	2015
The Headless Horseman	2016

Fantastically Funny Fantasy:

The Banned Underground Collection

Too many to list!

See www.thebannedunderground.com

CONTENTS

	Prologue	Pg 2
1	Chapter One	Pg 4
2	Chapter Two	Pg 25
3	Chapter Three	Pg 46
4	Chapter Four	Pg 63
5	Chapter Five	Pg 80
6	Chapter Six	Pg 98
7	Chapter Seven	Pg 118
8	Chapter Eight	Pg 147
9	Chapter Nine	Pg 167
10	Chapter Ten	Pg 185
11	Chapter Eleven	Pg 202
12	Chapter Twelve	Pg 219
13	Chapter Thirteen	Pg 241

Prologue

Mrs Gordone looked dispassionately at the portrait that stood on an artist's display easel in the front window of the shop. She regarded the picture called *'Portrait of a girl'* for a long drawn out moment. Then her gaze lingered on the stream of bright blood that slowly welled up from the canvas and dripped down the painting, over the frame, and pooled on the floor below the easel. Still without expression she walked to the desk on the other side of the room.

Without sitting down, she picked up the receiver of the telephone and dialled a number from memory. The dialling tone rang for a long time. A connection was made at last.

"Yes?" asked the voice at the far end of the line, without preamble.

"It's me. It's happened again."

"What has happened again?"

"'*Portrait of a Girl*'. Again. *You* know what."

There was a long pause, such a long silence that glaciers could have been born, grown to their full strength and finally melted away in the time taken for a reply.

"I see. Then I'm afraid she will have to be returned to the storeroom. Please clean up after her, and I will send someone to collect her picture."

"Thank you. Will there be a replacement for her?"

"Oh yes, there will be a replacement. Perhaps she should be covered over until my courier arrives with you to deliver that and collect her. I think that *The Unicorn* will make a suitable replacement for you. I will have him packaged up, the courier will deliver him at the same time."

There came a click, and the line was disconnected. Mrs Gordone replaced the handset, and walked to the shop's small storeroom. From a cupboard she withdrew a large linen cloth capable of wrapping and concealing the picture, a mop and a bucket. She filled the bucket with water and added a little bleach: then she walked purposefully toward the window.

Unnoticed as yet by the public filing through the arcade, past the window on their way to work, droplets of blood welled out from below the right hand of the girl and rolled down the canvas onto the frame of the portrait. They collected there and then dripped, one by one, into the slowly widening pool below the stand. Within her portrait, the girl stared serenely into her infinity.

Chapter One

The bell - attached in a rather flimsy fashion to the door frame - rang loudly as Sheila Balsam walked into the shop. She looked all around at the displays, with a casual interest, before wandering across to a case that displayed terracotta statues. The ceiling was low, the windows cluttered and dim, and Sheila had to peer through her glasses at the figurines.

"Are you interested in anything in particular?" she heard.

Sheila looked around, but the shop was empty, and she frowned, puzzled.

"Hello?" she asked in the general direction of the counter. Her frown eased, as a motherly lady emerged through a bead curtain close to the counter and smiled at her.

"Are you interested in anything in particular?" repeated the lady, in a rather refined accent that jarred slightly with her appearance. She was dressed in a velvet skirt, and a blouse that may once have looked like silk. A collection of beads and assorted necklaces hung around her neck, and Sheila wondered how she managed to walk so silently across the stained and varnished wooden floor.

"I wasn't really. I was just browsing, to be honest," admitted Sheila.

"This isn't really that sort of place, dear."

Sheila was taken aback. "What do you mean?"

"Well, most of the people who come through my door tend to know what they want, what they are looking for: and know that there's a good chance that they will find it here."

"So you don't get casual customers then? That must make it very hard."

The shopkeeper walked behind her counter, and leant on it with her arms crossed. Her long hair swung round to frame her face, and she smiled. "Not really. A few people are drawn in by the window display."

"I thought it was a bit cluttered myself," said Sheila.

"And that drew you inside, didn't it?"

Sheila smiled more politely, and turned back to examine the figureines displayed on the stand. They were all made of terracotta, and most resembled the fabled Chinese terracotta warriors. They were clearly individually made too, rather than cast from a mould and her interest sharpened.

"The warriors are rather interesting," she admitted.

"If I were you, I'd walk around to the other side of the stand. Unless I miss my guess, there is something there that will interest you very greatly."

Sheila looked curiously at the shopkeeper, who simply smiled back. She walked around to the other side of the display stand, and immediately her gaze was drawn to a unicorn statuette, about three feet high. Made of the same faded red terracotta as the other figures, it occupied most of the rear of the stand, and seemed to be examining her with blank, expressionless eyes.

"See? I said that you would like that!"

Sheila stretched out a hand, but the shopkeeper interrupted her. "No handling of the stock, unless you are serious in buying. These pieces are quite old, and can be fragile."

"But it looks like new. All the statues look like new. Are they real, then?"

"Of course they are real. What did you think, that I'd sell imitations?"

"But however did you get them? Wherever did you get them? Are they stolen?" Sheila regretted the last comment as soon as she had spoken, but the shopkeeper didn't take offence: in fact she laughed, a slightly disturbing sound in that hushed shop full of ancient relics from a forgotten past.

"No dear, they are not stolen. Everyone comes with a genuine certificate and proper documentation to show that we - and so you - are in possession of a lawfully exported object."

Sheila nodded, and her gaze was dragged back to the unicorn. His forelegs were raised from the ground, his muscled rear legs planted firmly and his wings outspread ready for flight. The horn was lowered, pointing forward in an attitude of defence - or maybe of attack.

"I'm attracted by this," she admitted. "I love dragons: but next to dragons, unicorns. Have you any dragons?"

The shopkeeper waved a hand dismissively, and leant forward slightly. "You don't want a dragon. I can see your nature, your aura: you don't want a dragon. You need a unicorn for your life path."

"Really?"

"Oh yes. A unicorn. Actually, I can see you with *that* unicorn. I think that he's been waiting for you."

Sheila examined the statue a little more closely. "He?" she asked. "Looks more like a 'she' to me."

"No. That unicorn is definitely a male, and as you live alone that will complement you."

"How did you know I live alone? Actually I don't. My mother lives with me."

"Not the same though, is it?" The shopkeeper sighed, a little theatrically. "I lived with my mother until she died. Actually, I still do as I keep her ashes near the fire. She always used to get chilly in an evening, and she likes to feel the warmth."

Sheila cast her a sharp glance to see if the shopkeeper was joking, but she seemed quite serious.

"You've no male partner: no don't look at me like that, any woman can tell," continued the shopkeeper. "So he'll just suit you perfectly. You will be amazed how your house will change when you move him in."

Impulsively Sheila made up her mind. "Done. I'll take her... him."

"Don't call him a her, he will take offence and things might not be so comfortable between you then."

"Oh, right." Sheila ignored the odd comment and rummaged in

her bag. She pulled out her purse. "How much did you say?"

"I didn't. But to you, let's see, £ 120 for delivery."

"How much delivery? And how much does the statue cost? I can take her…him… with me."

"No you cannot. You see, for security, we do not keep all the authenticity documents here at the shop. They are safely kept in our warehouse, and only join a piece when it is being transported. That is for our security and yours."

"I see," replied Sheila doubtfully.

"So you pay me the delivery charge now, and then pay for the piece itself later. Delivery will be the day after tomorrow, as it's a bit late in the afternoon today to organise the delivery for tomorrow."

"And how much will the cost be?" asked Sheila.

"You'll not be charged until you are happy with the piece, until you've bonded with him in your home."

"That's a bit odd, isn't it?" asked Sheila, taking her bank card from her purse. For a moment she wondered why on earth she was agreeing to buy something without knowing the cost: quite out of character for her. Then she glanced at the statuette, and promptly handed the card over to the shopkeeper.

"We are quite a traditional operation here. Customer satisfaction is very high on our priority list." The shopkeeper, with some difficulty, organised the card terminal and offered it to Sheila. She tapped in her security number: waited until instructed, and then removed her card.

"Please just fill in these delivery instructions." The shopkeeper handed Sheila a short form and an elderly pen.

"Let's see, full name..." Sheila filled in the details as she ran down the form. "Address... date and time of birth... place of birth..." what do you want these things for?"

"Security on delivery. Just to make sure that he has arrived at the right place, and with the right person. We did once have an accident, very difficult that was. Now we just like to check and make certain."

Sheila never gave true answers to such questions on websites, and so she copied down her normal alternative details, and returned the clipboard.

"Thank you. Delivery will be exactly at noon, on the day after tomorrow."

Sheila nodded, accepted her receipt for the payment, and still surprised with herself, left the shop to drive home.

The shopkeeper waited until she was again alone in the quiet shop and then picked up the handset of the elderly telephone. There was no dialling tone, but she spoke into it anyway. "She's gone. She's taken *The Unicorn*: delivery the day after tomorrow. Yes, I've got the necessary about her. I've got a good feeling about this one."

The silence at the other end of the telephone had a quality of finality, and the shopkeeper replaced the handset. From the far side of the shop she heard a small scraping noise, and she looked up sharply: but nothing moved or seemed out of place.

"Can't be too careful," she muttered to herself, and leaving the still and apparently empty shop, she went into the rear storeroom to select the appropriate packing case.

*

"You've bought a *what?*"

"A Unicorn, mother," explained Sheila, wearily. "It's made from terracotta, and it is very old."

"But why? And how can we possibly afford it?"

The accusation that she could not afford the statuette was actually a fair one, and Sheila bit her lip. The delivery fee had in fact almost emptied her bank account: luckily her salary would arrive in her account today, the day the unicorn was to be delivered.

Sensing a small victory, her mother continued, a shrewish tone evident in her voice. "You should ring them up, and cancel the delivery. Go on, do it now. They aren't here yet, they should give us the money back. Go on, you can do it right now."

Automatically, Sheila took a step towards the telephone, but then stopped. "I don't think that I will, mother. You see, I want this unicorn."

"What you want has nothing to do with anything. You'll

understand that when you get to my age!"

Sheila eyed her aging mother carefully. "You get the things you want, mother. You know you do."

"Ha! I want! If you only knew what I want, we'd be a lot happier, I can tell you."

"Mother…"

"Don't 'mother' me, my girl. Now go on, pick up that telephone. Right now."

Very reluctantly, Sheila picked up the telephone. Then she put it down again.

"What now?"

"The number. I need to get the phone number. It's in my other bag."

"Well be sharp then. Time's fleeting. Hurry up. Honestly, it's a very good thing for you that you've got me to live with you and stop you being so stupid all the time. If it wasn't for me we'd never have this nice little house to live in, would we?"

Sheila hurried out of the kitchen, and closed the door behind her, almost cutting off the flow of complaints. But something made her walk very slowly up the stairs to her bedroom. The delivery document with all the contact details on was not in that other handbag, it was in the waistband of her skirt, hidden by the long woolly top she wore around the house. She patted her waist to make sure and suddenly hurried up the last of the stairs, walked into her bedroom and closed the door firmly behind her.

She started counting, slowly, out loud. Earlier than she expected

- she had only reached forty - she heard her mother calling her name from the bottom of the stairs. Sheila carried on counting.

'Forty one...forty two... forty three...'

Now she could hear her mother coming up the stairs. Her mother's tread was always heavy, there was never any doubt in her mind who was on the stairs. Sometimes Sheila almost hoped for a burglar to be there, just for the novelty value. She pulled the delivery paper from inside the waistband of her skirt and looked at it.

"Fifty six...fifty seven... fifty eight...' Impulsively she flung herself backwards, and hid the delivery note under her pillow.

Her mother opened the door without knocking and stared at Sheila. "What do you think you are doing? Just sitting there?"

Sheila didn't answer.

"If you aren't going to do what I've told you, then you can stay there. If what I want means so little to you, you can stay there. But you will give me that paper now, and I will ring them up. Honestly, how they could take advantage of a young girl like you I've no idea! But they will listen to me."

Sheila nodded mutely. Then without raising her head, she said quietly: "I am thirty five years old mother. If I want to buy a statuette with my money, the money that I've earned by working, why shouldn't I?"

"Then you are too old for this to be teenage rebellion, aren't you?"

Sheila's mother held out her hand, the gesture imperious and demanding. Sheila shook her head. A tiny movement, but still a refusal.

Her mother suddenly sighed, and changed tack. She sat down on Sheila's bed, and put an arm round her daughter. "Sheila, darling. Haven't I always looked after you? Look where you would have been without me to help you. You'd have ended up with that awful boy, living a dreadful life somewhere horrid, instead of being in a nice house in this nice village. You'd be chained to a cooker all day - if not worse - just a household drudge. Look at what you have here."

"I'd have had my own life, mother."

"Now, none of that. You wouldn't have had a life at all. Here you have your nice job and we go places every month. Why, you even go out to places on your own, don't you? So you aren't the prisoner you would have been if you'd run off with that boy. You have your little car, don't you? You wouldn't be able to afford that if it wasn't for me."

Sheila nodded.

"So be a good girl for your mother and give me that delivery note."

Once again, Sheila shook her head. A more deliberate movement than before. Her mother looked around the room. As she insisted, it was very neat and tidy. As she expected of her daughter, the bed had been properly made that morning, the sheets tucked in firmly, the duvet squared and smoothed, the pillows neatly arranged. Or were they? One was less than perfectly aligned with the bed head. Smiling, Sheila's mother stood up and walked to the head of the bed. She lifted the nearest pillow with a sharp movement, and snatched the sheet of paper with satisfaction.

"See? You can't hide anything from your mother can you? Can you? *Can you?*"

"No, mother," replied Sheila in a small voice.

"Don't mumble at me. I won't have that."

"No, mother."

"Now, as you don't seem able to do even this simple little thing - lord knows how you keep that job when you can't even manage something as simple as this - *I* shall go and ring these people and tell them that they are not bringing this stupid thing into my home, and that they are to give us that money back straight away!"

Sheila's mother turned towards the door, animated by her small triumph over her daughter. "You really didn't need to make me come all this way up the stairs did you!" she complained.

Sheila looked at her hands, and said nothing. Leaving the bedroom door open, her mother walked out of the bedroom onto the landing, and grasped the banister. Then she paused. "Come down when you are ready to say 'sorry'!" she instructed.

Sheila sat on the end of her bed, still looking at her hands. A single tear slipped from the corner of her eye, kissed her cheek, and dropped onto her hand. Her mother's heavy footfalls descended the stairs, and she listened to every one. She heard the kitchen door open, and heard a gasp.

"Sheila! Sheila!" her mother shouted from the bottom of the stairs. "Get down here right away! Sheila!"

"What is it mother?" Sheila replied, listlessly.

"I never heard them come in. How dare they come in without knocking. Into my home!"

Sheila jerked her head up, her expression hopeful.

"It's an outrage! And it is only just midday. It's barely five minutes past midday."

Sheila ran out of her bedroom, and down the stairs, slipping on the last one in her haste.

"Be more careful, you silly girl! You could get yourself hurt behaving like that!" her mother said absently. "Now get in here and look at this!"

Sheila put one hand on the frame of the open kitchen door, to steady herself. She looked with wonder and delight at the wooden packing case that had appeared on the kitchen table. "My unicorn!" she exclaimed.

"An outrage!" insisted her mother. "How dare they come into my home without knocking, without my permission! How dare they! I shall complain in the strongest terms."

She turned to the telephone, and looking at the paper she held in her hand, she dialled the telephone number printed on the top. The ring tone ended, as the connection was made. "Hello? Hello!" she said fiercely, enjoying herself. "Hello? Will you please answer me at once!"

Sheila walked slowly all around the kitchen table. The packing case had a number - 10116 - stencilled on two sides of the case, but was otherwise unmarked. No fastenings or ties seemed to be fixed to it, and no delivery instructions or notes were with the case. She reached out and touched the packing case, and jumped slightly as if she had been shocked. She could hear her mother shouting into the telephone on the other side of the kitchen, but paid her no attention.

She gently grasped the lid with both hands, and pulled.. To her astonishment, the lid lifted easily as if it was not fixed in place. The sides of the packing case promptly fell away, banged onto the kitchen table and dropped to the tiled floor with a clatter. She stood there astonished, still holding the lid. Mrs Balsam stopped talking into the unreceptive silence of the telephone, and looked around.

"Sheila! Whatever have you done? How are we going to send it back now?"

"I didn't do anything, mother," replied Sheila. "I just touched the lid of the case, look!"

"I suppose you are going to tell me it fell apart of its own accord, are you? There's a wilful streak in you this morning, and I don't like it at all, my girl!"

Sheila did not reply. She turned the lid of the case over and over in her hands, examining it. "Was there no consignment note, mother?" she asked.

"No! And that's another thing. They answered the telephone, and didn't have the courtesy to even speak to me. I expect that some rude young man simply put the telephone down and walked away! I'll have a thing or two to say to them!"

"How will you do that, if they won't speak to you?" asked Sheila absently.

"Sheila!"

"You see mother, I was supposed to pay for the statuette when they delivered it. But how can I do that if there's no invoice or note?"

"There is that," agreed her mother. "There's no proof that it ever came here, is there? So how can you be expected to pay them?"

Sheila twisted round and placed the lid of the packing case on the worktop. Then she opened the kitchen drawer, and took out a big pair of kitchen scissors.

"I'll see if there's anything outside, or on the door," said her mother thoughtfully, and walked across the kitchen to the back door of the house. It was still locked. "Of course, they would not have come in through the garden," she said. "They must have come in through our front door, the scoundrels. Sheila, you really must learn to lock up properly! We could have been murdered in our beds, and it would be you to blame!"

"And not the murderers?" asked Sheila absently, looking at the bubble wrap packaging that covered the statuette so completely that it was obscured from view.

Her mother snorted, and walked out of the kitchen. Sheila heard her rattling the front door, which was held by both a Yale and a mortice lock. Shortly afterwards, her mother walked slowly back into the kitchen. Sheila was surprised to realise that her mother was looking very puzzled.

"That's very odd Sheila, the front door was locked, too."

"Yes," said Sheila, starting to cut away at the bubble wrap and the brown tape that held it in place. "I locked up when I came home, and neither of us have been outside since."

"What about the cat?"

"Molly uses the cat flap, as you know full well, mother."

"So if all the doors are locked, how did they get that in here? It wasn't here when we had breakfast and I was telling you off. It came in when I had to follow you up to your bedroom to get this paper." Sheila's mother waved the original delivery advice note as evidence.

"Well I don't know, as you know I was upstairs at the time."

Sheila continued cutting away at the bubble wrap, and one of the outstretched wings of the unicorn appeared. Gently she pulled at the packaging, smiling at the popping noises as several of the cells exploded under the pressure of her fingers.

"What an ugly thing," sneered Mrs Balsam.

"You can't see it yet, mother."

"I can see enough to know that I don't like it."

Gently Sheila unwrapped the material from the unicorn's head, struggling a little as the horn caught on the packing, and several louder pops from the bubble wrapping made her mother step back from the table.

"Look at his head," said Sheila. "Isn't he beautiful?"

Sheila's mother grabbed at the protective packaging and pulled at it forcefully. The statuette rocked, and Sheila gasped.

"Mother! Mother. Don't touch him." Her voice rose to a scream. "Don't you touch him! You are never to touch him!"

Sheila had never before raised her voice like that to her, and out of shock her mother needed a moment before responding. "Sheila! How dare you. Think of what you are saying! Think about who you are talking to! I'm your mother!"

The unicorn settled down on the kitchen table, and Sheila continued to carefully cut the packaging away from the legs. At last the final piece came away in her hand, and she cast it carelessly to the floor.

"I hope you are going to tidy all that up!"

"Yes, mother," said Sheila. Automatically she bent down to pick up the wrapping, but then stopped and straightened instead. She concentrated on the unicorn, and walked slowly around the table to admire the statuette.

"What's it made of then?" asked her mother, her curiosity finally defeating her desire for dominance of her daughter.

"Terracotta, mother. Like the famous Chinese warriors from the Emperor's Tomb."

"Tomb? This has been in a tomb?"

"I don't know."

"I really don't like it, Sheila."

Sheila looked at her mother with an unusual expression. "I don't care."

"Sheila, I'm serious. There's something about this thing."

"It's not a thing. It's a unicorn. *My* unicorn."

"I don't like the idea that this has been in a tomb."

"You aren't superstitious, mother. You are always telling me how that sort of stuff is just nonsense to frighten children, aren't you?"

"Sheila, I think I might be frightened of that."

Sheila looked at her mother with some interest. "Something I have frightens you, mother?"

Sheila's mother walked closer to the table, and stood beside her daughter. Together they regarded the unicorn. Horn raised threateningly, the terracotta eyes stared balefully across the kitchen.

Sheila smiled. "I think that he's quite lovely."

"Why do you say 'him?" Sheila's mother reached out gingerly towards the statuette, but Sheila seized her wrist. Surprised, her mother did not resist as Sheila pulled her mother's hand back, away from the unicorn.

"I said don't touch!" insisted Sheila in a cold manner. Then her voice reverted to her normal tone. "I don't know. It just feels right. Besides, can you imagine a woman containing so much power?"

They both looked at the statuette.

"I see what you mean, Sheila. How old is it?"

Sheila looked uncertain. "I don't think... I don't know. The shop said that it was very old and it feels old, wouldn't you say?"

"Oh yes, it looks old, all right."

"The shop said that it would come with certificates and papers that said how old it was, and that it was lawfully in private hands."

"Lawfully? So it's not only from a tomb, but it might have been stolen? Sheila, have you bought something that's been stolen from a tomb?"

"Mother, I told you, the shop said it was completely legitimate."

"Do you know what happens to people who buy things that have been stolen from tombs, Sheila?"

"Mother, you have been watching those horror films again, haven't you? You know your doctor said that you had to stop."

"He was just being stupid. But there was the Curse of Tutenkhamun... Lord Caernarvon, Howard Carter, all those others..."

"That is just silly. Those things aren't real."

"But he's real, Sheila. And he looks like he came from a tomb."

"Mother, get a grip on yourself. The unicorn is Chinese, and King Tut was Egyptian."

"Those foreigners are all the same to me. And their grave goods are best avoided."

"Well, you can't send him back because you haven't got the telephone number. I'm going to put him on that stand in the living room, the one near the TV."

"No, Sheila." Her mother started to regain her assurance. "I'm not having it near my TV, I'll not be able to watch it without feeling it's looking at me all the time. You can put it in the hall. Then if we do get burgled, it can terrify the living daylights out of the burglars, like it does to me."

Sheila nodded, and with some difficulty picked up the statuette, holding it carefully in her arms. She walked out of the kitchen, and missed her mother's sudden expression of relief. Below a window in the wide hall was a stand with a large plant pot. The pot held a lavender plant that Sheila had carefully grown from a cutting, nurturing it until it had grown and now occupied - if not filled- a large ornamental pot. Cradling the unicorn, Sheila lifted her right foot and kicked the plant pot from the stand. It tumbled to the floor, shattering and spreading compost across the polished wooden floor. Sheila gently put the unicorn down on the stand. She stepped back, treading on the plant as she did so, without noticing or caring. The unicorn reared on the stand, and she smiled in pleasure. Her hands and arms tingled, and Sheila felt slightly giddy: unexpected and unaccustomed ideas and feelings running through her thoughts.

Her foot moved, and a piece of broken plant pot clinked. Sheila blinked, and looked down at the plant below her feet. Surprised, she hurried down the hall back into the kitchen. Completely ignoring her mother's querulous demand, she picked up a dustpan and brush and a roll of black rubbish bags. She walked back to the front door, and started to sweep up the compost. The damaged plant she thrust into the rubbish bag without a second glance, and the compost followed. Sweeping furiously, she didn't notice her mother arrive to investigate.

"Sheila! What have you done? That was my favourite plant!"

"I must have knocked it over, mother."

"What do you mean? It was safely on that stand!"

"Well the unicorn is there now, so we don't need this plant anyway. I'm sorry about the pot."

"You never used to feel that way about plants. You bought that as a young seedling, ten years ago, for Mother's day!"

"And you complained at me for it. For days. I remember, mother."

Sheila swore as part of the broken plant pot cut her finger when she picked it up.

"Sheila! What have I told you about using such common language!"

"Sorry, mother," replied Sheila automatically.

Sheila's mother knelt down and started picking up bits of the pot, and putting them into the rubbish bag. "I never really liked the pot though," she said. "Why did you put that thing down facing the kitchen door? I'm going to feel it looking at me now whenever I come down the stairs or go in or out of the kitchen."

"I didn't," replied Sheila. "I set him down facing the front door, to repel intruders."

Kneeling down amongst the scattered earth and shards of broken pottery, the two women looked up at the terracotta unicorn as it reared above them on the display stand, the horn facing the kitchen door.

Chapter Two

Sheila woke suddenly in the middle of the night. She was never a very heavy sleeper, and every morning her bedclothes looked as if they had been tossed around by a giant mixing machine. What had disturbed her? She looked at the clock that stood on her bedside cabinet. The numbers normally sent a comforting crimson glow across her bed, but tonight they seemed unusually subdued. The time was half past three.

Sheila relaxed a little. It was not uncommon now for her mother to have to get up in the middle of the night. Either for some tablets: painkillers her mother always called them: or to use the toilet. Either occasion normally disturbed Sheila briefly. Tonight was clearly no different, and Sheila lay back down on her comfortable, comforting pillows, reassured that she knew what had awoken her. Her dreams had been - different and unsettling, containing memories of people and events that she would rather not have recalled - and she was not displeased to have awoken.

Her bedroom door was of course completely closed, but still she could see a bead of golden light around the frame. This meant that her mother had turned on the landing light, and was going downstairs to the kitchen. Sheila listened carefully as she heard her mother grumble something she couldn't make out, and carried on listening until she heard her mother's heavy footfalls carry on along the landing, past her door, and start down the stairs towards the kitchen.

Sheila rolled over and buried her head under the covers, waiting for sleep to return and overwhelm her again. To count sheep was a traditional cure for lying awake, and she tried to think of sheep jumping a fence The atmosphere of the house suddenly felt different, inexplicably changed. Not sheep: unicorns. She smiled to herself, and started counting unicorns to herself. Not jumping fences or gates: too mundane for such a noble exotic animal, she felt. Instead as she drifted back to the realm of Morpheus, she saw terracotta unicorns marching in ranks across a wide, green field, stamping, prancing, then narrowing their column of march as they passed through a sudden defile into a ravine. The walls of the ravine rose, but still the unicorns marched on, their advance implacable, unstoppable. Now the upper walls of the cliffs grew together and the unicorns dwindled, became one unicorn charging forward into an increasingly lightless cavern. Sheila felt fearful for them, for these noble creatures, now merged into one great animal. Ahead stood a dark figure with one hand raised in admonition, yet without fear the unicorn resolutely carried on and on and on and on into the darkness. Her fading memory of the dream was of the unicorn lowering his horn and charging the figure before him. As the horn pierced the breast of the dark figure, Sheila thought she heard a cry. She was asleep.

Sheila's mother sighed heavily as she looked at her illuminated bedside clock. One of the less pleasant things about getting old was her growing need to get up in the middle of the night. Accustomed to an orderly, controlled life her body's recent independence in this matter was a source of annoyance for her.

Her bedroom window was open, and she could hear the sudden, urgent howling of a cat fighting. The sound stopped, and she frowned in exasperation at being disturbed. She found it harder and harder to get back to sleep these days. The cat fight ended abruptly, and the howling stopped. Mrs Balsam snorted her annoyance.

A much more immediate annoyance of course was Sheila's sudden insistence on keeping the statuette of the unicorn. She could not think what had got into her normally complaisant daughter. This was more important than the pain in her back: she was used to that. After mulling the matter over for a while, her back pain became too insistent for her to ignore it further and she reluctantly accepted that without any pain relief medication she was not going to get any further sleep that night.

With another heavy sigh she swung her legs out of bed. Sitting up and bending forward to search for her slippers, she hissed with the jolt of pain from her lower back. "I hate getting older," she said very quietly, perhaps in the hope that she would not hear herself say it.

She didn't need to turn on her bedroom lamp to make her way to the door, but once that was open the darkness was too much for her to feel safe walking across the landing and down the stairs. The switch for the light that hung at the top of the stairs was beside her bedroom door. She fumbled awkwardly with her left hand, but then found the switch and turned on the light. There was a brief scuffling sound at the bottom of the stairs so she walked across to the banisters and looked down into the hall. The kitchen door was open, and a shadow moved.

"It's Molly," she thought. A moment later she heard the cat flap open and close, and relaxed. Only then when she relaxed did she realise that she had been tense.

"This is silly," she said aloud to herself. She paused for a moment, but could hear nothing from Sheila's room, and the rest of the house was quiet too. She took a firm hold of the banister rail and started down the stairs. She counted each step on the way down as was her habit. At the bottom of the stairs she stopped and looked along the hall towards the front door. The single bulb at the top of the stairs cast an adequate yet dim light along the hall. Nothing moved, and she was unaccountably relieved. The unicorn stood on the stand near the window, facing the front door just as they had left it. After the discussion over the broken plant pot Sheila had picked up the unicorn and turned it to face the front door. She had re opened the cut on her finger whilst doing so and had asked her mother to get a cloth to wipe the blood from the unicorn's horn. Her mother recalled walking out of the kitchen with a damp cloth, only for Sheila to tell her that it wasn't needed now.

"Too late," Sheila had said to her mother. "It's all gone now."

Now in the dark of the night Sheila's mother found herself wondering where the blood had gone. "Of course," Sheila will have wiped it off herself," she decided. "She just did that to be annoying."

She turned away from the front door and the hall and walked into the kitchen through the open door. Behind her she fancied that she heard a noise. She took a deep breath before walking back into the hall, and chided herself for being silly. She turned on the hall light too and looked all around. She examined the position of the unicorn statue. Was it her fancy or was it suddenly out of its previous position? Of course it was her fancy. But when she walked back into the kitchen she still pulled the door shut behind her.

Mrs Balsam turned on the kitchen light and walked across to the cupboard where she kept the medicines. She opened the cupboard door, then turned back to the sink. Taking a glass from the side of the sink, she rinsed it under the tap and then filled it with water. Setting it down on the worktop with a click, she reached into the cupboard and pulled out the packet of pain relief capsules. She pulled some of her painkillers from the packet, and put them in her mouth. She reached for the glass, and stopped as she heard a click. Was that the glass clicking on the worktop, or was it the sound of the kitchen door opening? She grasped the glass firmly, and turned to face the door. It was ajar, but not properly open.

"I must have not closed it properly," she said aloud. "It's that statue thing. It's really upset me, as has Sheila's behaviour over it, and I'm thinking silly things."

She drank a little of the water, wincing at the acrid taste of the tablets now that they had sat in her mouth for a few moments. She put the glass down, and as she did so the door moved slightly. "I may be getting old, but I'm not senile!" she said firmly, then walked across the kitchen floor to the door. She took hold of the handle, and pulled the door open.

She gasped as a dark shadow rose up before her, the horn on its forehead almost scraping the ceiling.

"No..." she managed.

Sheila's mother stepped backwards across the kitchen floor. The ceiling light failed and went out. The shadow tilted its head forward to enter the kitchen and the bright glow from its red eyes became the only illumination in the kitchen. In that glow she could see the horn on the shadow's forehead swing downwards. It pointed directly at her as the shadow rushed forward: she wondered if she would have time to scream, and decided to try anyway.

I was making breakfast the next morning when my telephone rang. Although I had no way of knowing that anything was wrong, the tone seemed to have an ominously insistent quality and I was unexpectedly nervous about taking the call. My premonition was confirmed when a sobbing scream came out of the earpiece before I even had time to answer.

"Mister Jones! Mister Jones, please, please, help. It's my mother!"

Even though her tones were distorted by both the telephone and by the emotion evident in her voice, I had no difficulty in recognising the voice of the younger of the two ladies who lived next door to me. But I thought it was wise to be sure.

"Sheila Balsam? Sheila, is that you?"

"Yes! *Yes!* Please, Mister Jones, just come round at once. I need help."

Obviously she was in some distress, so I left the kitchen in such a hurry that I forgot to take the toast out of the toaster. I suppose that I am lucky I didn't start a fire that way. It would not have taken me very long to walk down the path leading from my door to the front gate, and then back down the path to the front door of my neighbour's house. However it seemed sensible to jump over the low fence between our properties. I was in such a hurry that I didn't pay enough attention to what I was doing and ended up on my knees in my neighbours' flowerbed. When I knocked on the door, my trousers were muddy from the knee down. Sheila took no notice.

As soon as she opened the front door, she grabbed my hand. Tears streamed down her face, and she was sobbing so hard that I could not understand her properly at first.

"Mister Jones! Thank you! Quick, it's my mother!"

Sheila pulled me down the hall towards the kitchen, and I stopped abruptly at the open door. The sight was appalling.

"Help her, help me," Sheila pleaded.

I took one long look at her mother lying on the floor of the kitchen. I didn't need to get closer to see that she was dead. The blood that had spread out and pooled around her had dried on the floor. I turned back to the hall to shut out Sheila's view of her mother, and pulled the kitchen door closed. I felt sick, and couldn't imagine what this young girl must be feeling.

"Aren't you going to help her?" shouted Sheila, and pushed at me with surprising strength.

"Sheila, come into the living room and sit down," I said. "Your mother has gone beyond that sort of help. Who have you rung?"

"Just you, Mister Jones. I didn't know who else to call."

She collapsed against me, and I helped her into the living room and into a chair. "Where's your telephone, Sheila?"

"It's, it's in the kitchen."

I didn't feel like opening that door again. "Do you have another one?"

She shook her head.

"A mobile phone?"

"Yes. Yes!"

Sheila jumped out of the chair, and scrabbled at a bag that lay on the floor near the window. She pulled out a mobile phone, and thrust it at me with shaking hands. I guided her into the chair again and she covered her face with her hands and dissolved into tears. I walked back into the hall and closed the door behind me. Using a mobile phone is a novelty for me, but this one was easy to work and I was able to dial the emergency services without too much difficulty.

"Which service do you require?" asked the operator.

"Ambulance, please: and police. No, police first."

"Connecting you now."

The police answered immediately.

"I'm reporting a death," I said.

The tone of the police response team member was matter of fact and without emotion, as she asked for the appropriate details of address and my personal details. "Are you sure that the lady is dead?" she asked me. "Have you checked?"

I swallowed. "She is lying on the floor with a big hole in her chest. There's blood all around her, and it has dried."

"But have you checked to see if she is still alive?"

"No. I didn't go further into the kitchen than I had to."

"The response teams have been alerted, sir. But I should ask you to just look and see if this lady is still alive. Try not to disturb anything around, but we need to see if there is any emergency aid that you can give her whilst we wait for the response team to reach you. Please stay on this line, and tell me what you are doing."

"I don't want to do this," I said into the phone.

"Mister Jones, what's happening?" shouted Sheila from the living room.

"Her daughter is here, and very distressed," I whispered into the phone.

"How old is she?" asked the police support worker.

"Late twenties, I think. Maybe early thirties."

"Thank you."

The speaker of the mobile telephone was faint but I could clearly hear the operator's fingers tapping information into her keyboard.

"I'm opening the kitchen door, and walking into the kitchen," I said.

The keyboard continued to rattle.

"I'm going to try and... no, no, I'm sorry. She's obviously dead. In fact..."

I pulled the phone away from my face, bent over and was violently sick into a corner of the kitchen. I could hear the police support worker calling my name, but I ignored her. I turned and stumbled back out of that awful room and thankfully closed the door on the sight of the dreadfully dead body of my neighbour. I must confess that I have never felt so relieved to hear the intrusive, commanding wail of police vehicles before, and I hurried to open the front door to greet the arrivals.

The police cars turned off their wailing sirens and stopped outside the house. Moments later, and an ambulance arrived from the opposite direction. I watched two plain clothes policemen leave the first car. Two uniformed officers joined them, and I was very relieved to see that one was a woman, for that would relieve me of the need to tend to the distressed daughter I had left sobbing in her living room.

I recognised the senior policeman, having met him before. As the first of the policemen, Detective Inspector Peake, strode down the path to the front door he looked properly at me and recognised me in return. His step checked and then he continued.

"Mister Jones," he greeted me with a noticeable lack of warmth in his voice.

"Inspector Peake," I acknowledged him. "Sergeant Wilson, I greeted the other plain clothes officer, whom I had also met before.

"Where?" was all Inspector Peake asked me.

"In the kitchen," I replied. "Her daughter is in the living room, and quite distressed. Probably your lady colleague here could be of assistance to her?"

Inspector Peake turned and nodded at the young constable. "Your job, Erica."

"Yes, sir," she replied. She looked at me. "Where is the young lady?"

"First door on the left," I replied. "At the end of the hall is the kitchen, where…" my voice tailed off. Peake nodded again at the constable, and she walked down the hall, and into the living room. She closed the door firmly behind herself, and I silently wished her the best of luck. The other young constable positioned himself at the front door. The ambulance crew followed the policemen down the path, and Inspector Peake looked at me with a stony expression. "You sure she's dead, Mister Jones?"

I nodded.

Peake turned to the ambulance crew. "Please check her, but be careful, you know what I mean?"

The ambulance crew nodded. I stood aside and they walked purposefully past me, down the hall and into the kitchen. Inspector Peake and his colleague, Sergeant Wilson waited silently. After a moment, the medics walked out of the kitchen and beckoned to the policemen. Inspector Peake walked into the hall, and looked around, then walked down the hall to the medic.

Sergeant Wilson stood beside me, but made no attempt at conversation. I watched his eyes: he too was examining the hall, and I saw him stare with interest at a scattering of soil across one side of the carpet that covered the floor. I looked down the hall, and saw one of the ambulance crew shake his head firmly. Then they both came back up the hall, and walked slowly past me without speaking. They returned to their vehicle, to wait.

Inspector Peake called to me from the end of the hall: he still had not actually walked into the kitchen. "Mister Jones! Please come here."

As he had been polite enough to say please, I walked slowly towards him. I was aware that the stolid figure of Sergeant Wilson was very close behind me.

"Mister Jones, you went into the kitchen?" asked Peake.

"Yes," I told him. "But only at the request of the emergency operator."

"Yes, I understand that. Did you identify the body? There will of course be a formal identification later, but just for now? That way I do not - yet- have to speak to the distressed lady in the living room."

"Yes, Inspector. That is my neighbour. Mrs Balsam."

"When you went into the kitchen, to see if Mrs Balsam was, well, still alive: did you touch anything? Did you disturb anything?"

"No, Inspector. Although I was very sick in one corner."

I could sense a hint of suppressed laughter coming from behind my left shoulder, and strove to ignore it.

"Can you please tell me how you came to be here, Mister Jones?" asked Inspector Peake, in a neutral tone. We had met a few times before, and I knew that the inspector looked upon me with a mixture of suspicion and dislike. In fact, I was surprised by the lack of hostility in his voice.

"Mrs Balsam is - was- my next door neighbour. Her daughter rang me, asking for help: I cam round and found her, well, you can see for yourself. I rang the police immediately."

"I see," said the Inspector thoughtfully. "Did you hear a disturbance in the night?"

"No," I replied.

"We'll need a statement from you, of course. I must ask you to come to the police station and we will take a formal statement there."

I nodded, resigned. I had expected nothing else.

Sergeant Wilson, who was still standing very close to me, spoke over my shoulder. "Sir, the SOCO team is here."

A group of men in white coverall suits were clustered at the front door, awaiting clearance to enter and start their grim work.

"Right," replied Inspector Peake decisively. "We'll need to clear the area to let them get to work. Wilson, you can arrange to take Miss Balsam to the station with Erica. We'll need to get her formal statement, so we might as well do it there. Mister Jones here can come with me."

Wilson looked as if he might object, but changed his mind. "Yes sir." It was clear to me from his expression that a car journey with a near hysterical woman did not appeal to him.

"Privilege of rank!" said Inspector Peake. He took my arm and ushered me down the hall towards the front door, past the SOCO team. "In you go," he said to them as we passed, and they set off with their cases of equipment. "Jim," he addressed the leader of the team: "All the doors, windows and entrances too."

"Of course," replied the SOCO team leader, although I thought I caught a glimpse of irritation in his face at the reminder.

Inspector Peake ushered me out to the leading police car, and from behind I could hear Sheila being escorted out of the house by Sergeant Wilson and the woman police officer.

*

The SOCO team leader watched the group leave the house with some relief. He hated being watched whilst at work. He turned to one of the team. "Jane - get some tape across the front door. We don't want anyone" - he paused and waved dismissively at the uniformed constable guarding the front door - "getting in here. Tread carefully down the hallway. There's some scattered stuff there we'd better log." The junior SOCO officer nodded, and walked carefully down the hallway. She brushed against the unicorn and exclaimed.

"What have you done?" demanded her team leader.

"Cut myself on this thing, Jim. Odd, it doesn't look sharp anywhere."

"Well get outside and get a plaster on the cut. Then you can take photos of the hall and brush the front door before the deceased has been removed. Peake will be looking for evidence of access - or lack of evidence, if you follow me..."

"Yes, Jim."

Jim looked at the two remaining team members waiting beside the kitchen door. "Let's start with the photos. Then we can get the body out of the way and really get to work."

His team nodded, and without speaking they set down their cases and took out cameras. The body was photographed from several angles, with particular attention paid to the damage to her chest and to the clear damage to the kitchen unit immediately behind her. They worked respectfully but thoroughly, and Jim waited patiently. At last they were satisfied, and Jim walked purposefully to the front door. He beckoned the ambulance crew, and they arrived with a wheeled stretcher. Efficiently the late Mrs Balsam was transferred to the stretcher, and taken away. Jim breathed a sigh of relief.

"OK, now let's get on. Jack: you do the window and the back door: Phil - you can dust the worktops and kitchen units around the impact area and collect samples from the dried blood. When I've checked on the front door and hallway, I'll do the door here." Satisfied that his team did not need his immediate supervision, Jim returned to the hall, and moved carefully towards the front door.

"Jane, have you moved this pot thing?"

"No, Jim. Haven't touched it. Still don't know how it cut me." Jane was crouched down on the floor on the other side of the hall, carefully scraping samples of the scattered soil into an evidence bag. Her camera lay on the floor and Jim picked it up. He looked at the last photographs on the screen, and then studied them more carefully.

"Well you must have done."

"Haven't touched it, Jim. I've just started to collect samples of this soil before dusting the front door for fingerprints."

"Well, look at this. In this picture that I took a few minutes ago that whatsit thing is facing the front door. Look. There's the spike."

Jane looked at the photograph of the unicorn, and then the two SOCO officers stared at the statuette of the unicorn. The horn faced down the hall towards the kitchen. "It's moved all right," agreed Jane. "But I never touched it."

"Don't be bloody silly. It's not going to move about on its own, is it? That will be enough of the soil for the report. The front door is a long shot as there's no sign of a forced entry, but we will need to dust it anyway."

"Yes, Jim," said Jane in a subdued voice.

Jim regarded the unicorn. "Not the thing I'd have in my

hallway."

"Perhaps it's there as protection against intruders?" suggested Jane, opening her case and taking out the dusting powder for identifying fingerprints.

"Scare them away by being ugly? Actually, I've had a thought. That spike. Make sure that you check it for blood."

"It's already had some of mine this morning. I bled quite a bit at first from that cut it gave me."

Jim looked more closely at the unicorn's horn. "Where? I can't see any blood here at all. No sign of anything on it. Well, check it anyway." He reached out to touch the figurine, then at the last minute thought better of it and pulled his hand away. For a moment he thought that the unicorn trembled on the stand.

"That stand actually looks a bit unsteady to me. I'd swear it wobbled just then, Jane. So watch it. I don't want to have to field complaints you've broken the thing, OK?"

"Yes, Jim." Jane turned her attention to the front door.

Jim looked again at the unicorn, then snorted and shook his head. He walked back to the kitchen door. He started by using the fingerprint powder on the light switch beside the door, and inspected the results carefully. "Too many touches, too smudged to get anything there," he muttered and then turned the lights on. Even in the daylight, such as it was in this dark time of the year, shadows shifted at the corners of his vision and despite his long experience he felt uncomfortable.

"Is it me, or is it a bit cold in here?" he asked his fellows in the kitchen.

"Yeah, it is a bit, Jim. You should have put those thermals on for a job this time of year," replied Jack.

"Having the front door open won't help, but at least we're not outside," offered Phil. He sat back on his heels and looked at the marks on the kitchen cupboards. "You know what? It looks to me like she was impaled on something. Went right through her, then scraped its way all the way down the cupboard."

"Nasty," agreed Jack. "Back door is locked and undamaged, Jim. I've dusted the inside, want me to do the outside?"

"Yes, of course. There's no sign of a forced entry - I've looked upstairs - so that means whoever did this either opened a door or had a door opened for them. Have you logged the prints from the windows?"

"Taken and recorded them all, Jim. I know they'll need to be scanned, but I'd already put money against there being anyone but the owners on there."

Jim shivered again, and knelt down to attend to the handle of the door between the hall and the kitchen. The atmosphere suddenly thickened, and the shadows seemed to grow around him, before shifting and collecting in the corner beside him, becoming darker and more dense. Jim turned his back on the corner and concentrated harder on collecting the prints from the door handle. The dark shadow in the corner changed shape as he moved, then slowly started to grow upon the wall - to grow up the wall. Jim worked on carefully, all his attention now on the door handle.

"Jim," called Phil from the kitchen. "This pile of vomit. You want me to log it?"

"You can do, but I think we already have it identified as that bloke from next door. Better get a sample though or Peake will be unhappy."

"Right. Not surprised he was sick, really. Whatever went through her went pretty deep into that cupboard door. I'm a bit amazed it wasn't pulled right off its hinges. Wouldn't like to meet whatever that was myself."

Behind the SOCO team leader the shadow on the wall became darker still. The long spike or horn growing from the top of its head became harder, more defined, in some way quite clearly both pointed and above all else, sharp. A faint red glow near the top of the shadowed figure suggested eyes. The horn began to dip towards Jim's back. The glow brightened, became two oval red eyes with black-slits for pupils. They focussed entirely upon Jim and glittered with malice.

Jim exhaled, his breath visible in the cold air surrounding him. Still facing the door he stood up and moved around to the other side of the door, his back now to the kitchen. On the wall, the shadow halted, and then moved slightly. The horn now faced the kitchen door.

"Bet it could go right through an internal door," Phil said. "Especially cheap doors like these. Did you know that inside they are just cardboard?"

"Mmmmm" replied Jim, busy with the dusting powder. He rubbed the bottom of his back, stood up and walked to the sink. "I must be getting old," he grumbled. "Every time I spend time crouched down like that, my back gives me hell."

In the hall, the shadow horn paused and then straightened. The shadow on the wall wavered and lost form before diminishing. The red eyes lasted longest, but at last they too faded.

"Goes with the job, Jim," said Jack cheerfully. "Here, it's actually warmer outside here than in that kitchen."

"Not hard, that," muttered Jim. He eased his back again, and then returned to work on the door to the hall. As he finished, Jane returned from the front door.

"All done," she told her team leader.

"We're all about finished too," Jim decided. "Have either of you two anything you want to check, add to the log, or examine again?"

Phil shook his head, and Jack came back inside the kitchen. He closed and locked the back door of the house. "Me neither," he said.

"Then we will pack up. Close up your cases, make sure you have all the samples logged and the print records secure. Powder brushes in the separate bag for disposal back at the office."

The SOCO team did not look as if they needed that reminder, but chose not to comment. After a brief flurry of activity, the team left the kitchen. Powder of various colours was scattered freely around all the surfaces, but it was not part of their job description to clean up or tidy up after their work.

"Did you examine that unicorn thing?" Jim asked Jane.

"Yes. Funny, I know that I bled over it, Jim, but when I looked I couldn't see any trace at all."

"Something must be about somewhere. When we get back to the lab, do not forget to leave a sample of your blood, logged and tagged, so that if it comes out anywhere we will be able to eliminate you rather than have Inspector Peake hauling you off for the third degree!"

"Do I tell the uniforms that they can start their search now, Jim?" asked Jane.

Jim took one last look around the silent house. "Yes, let them at it," he agreed.

The SOCO team walked past the unicorn on its stand, resolutely facing the front door and left the house. They closed the front door behind them, and the unicorn trembled slightly, as if disturbed by the vibration.

Chapter Three

I sat behind the grey table that comprised most of the furniture in the interview room, and stared morosely at the cold cup of tea before me. I had not felt much desire to drink it when it was hot, and now that it was cold I felt even less enthusiasm.

"The catering hasn't improved since I was last in here," I told the young constable assigned to ensure that I stayed in the room.

"Sorry about that," he replied. his insincerity clear. "It's no better for us, either."

I stretched on the hard plastic chair, and sighed. At that point, the door opened and Inspector Peake entered the room, followed by Sergeant Wilson.

"I'm sorry to have kept you, Mister Jones," said Inspector Peake. His apology was even less sincere than that of the constable a few moments earlier.

"I'm sure that you have been busy, Inspector."

The two police officers sat down on the other side of the table. Peake opened the file he was holding, and Sergeant Wilson opened two new cassette tapes and placed them into the recording machine that sat on the end of the table. Once he had finished and set the recordings in motion he proceeded to give me the latest Official Caution.

"Please identify yourself for the tape," asked Inspector Peake.

I gave my full name, address and date of birth.

"Now, Mister Jones," Peake began."

I held up a hand to stop him. "First, Inspector, how is my neighbour?"

"Miss Balsam is quite upset, Mister Jones. We have a doctor with her now, so we thought we would take your evidence about this morning before we talk to her."

"Do you need to interview her? She has just lost her mother, Inspector. Quite appallingly, too. She must be awfully upset."

Sergeant Wilson looked a little grim. "Mister Jones, do you want to know how often - statistically - such murders are committed by members of the family?"

I opened my mouth to respond, and then realised that I would only look very foolish and naïve, as he was undoubtedly correct.

Peake smiled, rather sadly, I thought. "Now, Mister Jones, will you please relate the events of this morning? I will make it clear that at this point you are not suspected of any involvement and your statement is that of a witness to the events."

I had met Inspector Peake before, I had been interviewed by him before (although I had always been entirely innocent of any wrongdoing), and I knew that at the very least he viewed me with considerable suspicion. But my part in the events was simple, and I told him so.

"Inspector, I was in my kitchen this morning making breakfast, when my telephone rang. I am sure that the telephone company will be able to confirm the time of the call for you."

"It may be news to you Mister Jones, but even in this day and age it is not that easy to obtain that information," Wilson told me. I really did not believe him, but continued.

"The caller was the young lady who lives next door to me with her mother."

"Names for the tape please?" asked Sergeant Wilson.

"They are a Mrs Florence Balsam and a Miss Sheila Balsam."

"No one else?"

"Not to my knowledge, no."

"Boyfriends?" asked Inspector Peake, making notes

"I don't keep a watch on them, Inspector. I'm not GCHQ or James Bond, you know."

"Go on, please, Mister Jones."

"Miss Balsam was hysterical. She asked me to come round next door immediately as something had happened to her mother. She was so clearly distressed that naturally, I did."

"Front door or back?" asked Sergeant Wilson.

"Front door. There is a high hedge between our houses at the back, and it would have been difficult to get there quickly."

"OK. Front door."

"I knocked, and Miss Balsam unlocked the door..."

"It was locked then?" asked Inspector Peake in such a neutral manner that I knew he was very interested in my reply.

"Yes. I heard a key turn in the door before Miss Balsam opened it. She told me her mother was in the kitchen, and asked me to help. I walked down the hallway to the kitchen door, and looked inside."

"Did you touch anything in the hall?" asked Sergeant Wilson.

"No."

They waited, silent, for me to continue.

"It was immediately clear that her mother must… must.. must have… must be dead."

I swallowed and drank some of the awful tea without noticing the taste. "Naturally I pulled Miss Balsam away from the sight into her living room, and rang the emergency services at once."

"That call is logged and recorded, yes," said Sergeant Wilson.

"So as you know, I was asked to check that Mrs Balsam was dead. That was quite upsetting."

Neither police officer showed any sympathy for me there.

"I'm afraid that having to get close to the body made me sick."

That got me no sympathy either.

"Actually, that's contaminating a crime scene, and potentially a criminal offence," Inspector Peake told me.

Sergeant Wilson was a little more sympathetic than his superior. "You formally identified the body at the scene as that of your next door neighbour, Mrs Florence Balsam?"

"Yes. Yes, sergeant, I did. That was when you got there, as you know."

"What had you been doing in the meantime?" asked Wilson.

"Trying to comfort Miss Balsam," I replied.

Inspector Peake did show a little sympathy for me there. "Not easy. She is clearly distressed. From your experience of their home, did you notice anything odd, unusual or out of place?"

"Inspector, I was a long way from being a regular visitor. They bought the house four years ago, and I think I have been round to visit them no more than twice."

"They didn't like you?"

"They kept themselves to themselves, Inspector. They didn't have many visitors, and I don't think that they went out much. Miss Balsam works of course, but other than that, no."

"You called the emergency services from which telephone?" asked Inspector Peake.

"Miss Balsam had a mobile in her bag and I used that. I had hoped to avoid going into the kitchen, which is where they keep their ordinary phone. The landline."

"Did you go into any other rooms in the house?"

"Only the hall, the living room and the kitchen."

"Did you hear, or were you aware, of anyone else present in the house?"

"No, Inspector. Certainly no one came or left before the police and the ambulance crew arrived."

"Mister Jones, if you were comforting a distressed girl in the living room, how can you be sure?"

"The door was open, as I didn't want to be shut in with her on my own. I could see out of the door, and the stairs and the hall were in clear view. No one could have come down the stairs to leave without me seeing or hearing, and there are no other rooms."

"A cellar?" asked Peake.

"Oh. I hadn't thought. I don't think they have one, Inspector. I have in my house, but the door is in the hall next to the kitchen door. I didn't notice such a thing, but of course I may be mistaken. I wasn't really looking at the time."

Inspector Peake made a note on his pad, put the pad into his file, and closed it. He nodded to Sergeant Wilson, who turned towards the tape machine.

"Interview terminated," Wilson said. He looked at his watch and confirmed the time. Then he removed the cassettes, placed them into separate bags, labelled them carefully and passed one to me. "For your growing collection," he said.

"That's it?" I asked.

"Yes, you have been very helpful, Mister Jones, thank you."

Inspector Peake stood up. "Wrong place, wrong time again, Mister Jones? You have a bad habit of that, don't you?"

"I think perhaps I'm very unlucky, Inspector," I replied. "Do I get a lift home?"

"Atkins here will see to it." Peake looked at the constable. "Take Mister Jones home, please. We won't need him again today."

"Yes, sir," replied the constable. He looked at me. "This way out, sir."

"Mister Jones knows the way out, Atkins," said Peake drily.

The constable gave me a professionally blank look and opened the door. I walked out of the interview room. The corridor outside had not improved since my last visit to the police station, and I was pleased to leave. As I walked past the next room, I could see through the open door that Sheila was sitting at the table there. I was about to halt and speak to her, but with a gentle pressure on my arm Atkins urged me past the door. Sheila did not look up and see me, so I made no protest.

*

The doctor attached to the police station walked into the interview room and sat down opposite Inspector Peake. The Inspector looked up from his notes of the interview with Mister Jones. "Well?" he asked.

"You can talk to her," agreed the doctor. "Just take a little care, she's a bit distressed. And to me she seems very fragile."

"If she's done a Lizzie Borden, I'm not surprised," agreed Peake.

"Is she a suspect?" asked the police doctor.

"Not yet. But she was found with her mother dead. Inside their home. All the doors and windows were locked. So at the very least, there are questions to be asked. And right now she's going nowhere until she's answered some."

"Yes, I understand. But be cautious, Inspector. It won't help you if she collapses."

"Real or fake?" asked Sergeant Wilson, his years of cynicism showing.

"With her, I don't think you'd be able to tell the difference, Sergeant."

"She's a good actor, you think?" asked Inspector Peake, his interest quickening.

"No, I just think she is a bit unbalanced."

"Is that a formal diagnosis, doctor?"

"Of course not, Inspector. But you have on your hands a young woman in a highly emotional state. If you want some accuracy out of her, you need to tread carefully and sympathetically."

Sergeant Wilson opened his mouth to make a sarcastic comment, but caught his superior's eye and changed his mind. Inspector Peake stood up. "Is she fit to talk to me? Yes or no?"

"That is a 'yes' Inspector," replied the doctor.

"Then let's see for ourselves what this hothouse flower has to say for herself, shall we? Come on, Wilson."

Leaving the doctor still sitting at the table, Peake and Wilson left the room and walked a few strides down the corridor. Outside the door, Peake stopped, and pulled Wilson close so that he could whisper in his ear.

"You can take the lead on this one, Wilson. You come across more fatherly than I do, and it might help."

Sergeant Wilson nodded, and led the way into the interview room. Sheila looked up, her eyes puffy and red from weeping. Wilson sat down at the table, and dealt with the recording machine. He unwrapped two new tapes, inserted them into the machine, and switched it on.

"What's all this for?" asked Sheila.

"Technology, Miss. Helps us to get all the witness statements right," said Wilson.

"Oh. For a moment, I thought that you thought I could..."

"Miss, we've found your mother killed. It's our job to try and find out why - and who, so we'll need to take a lot of statements, and this makes our life easier."

"Oh."

"For the tape, could you please give us your name and address?"

Sheila did that, and Inspector Peake spoke for the first time.

"Also present are Detective Inspector Peake and Sergeant Wilson and Constable Erica Lewis. Miss Balsam, if you don't mind, we will do the interview under caution. It doesn't mean anything, just makes it official. But because of that, we have to ask you if you would like a duty solicitor present?"

Sheila looked bemused. "I haven't done anything, so it doesn't matter."

Wilson read out the caution, and then opened his file. Inspector Peake opened his notepad, and prepared to jot down some details.

"Miss Balsam, we'd like to start by saying how sorry we are for your loss, and how sorry we are that we have to put you through this ordeal," Wilson said.

Sheila just nodded.

"Now, I have to take you through the day. I know this is going to be distressing, but it has to be done."

"I understand," replied Sheila, in a small voice.

"Just for the tape, would you mind speaking up a bit for the next questions?"

"Sorry, I'm sorry. It's just all so distressing, you understand? I almost don't believe it happened at all."

"Could you tell me what happened this morning?" asked Sergeant Wilson.

"Must I, sergeant?" Sheila started crying again, and wiped her eyes with a tissue from her handbag.

"Please, Miss Balsam."

"From,... from when?"

"How about from when you got up this morning? What woke you up?"

"My alarm, as normal. I was supposed to be going to work. But, well…"

"So, you awoke. What then?"

"Sergeant! There are some things a lady isn't going to say!"

"Right, OK, we can move on," agreed Wilson. Inspector Peake looked as if he was about to say something, and Wilson looked enquiringly at his superior. Peake however elected to stay quiet. "After that?" asked Wilson.

"Well, it was time to get up so I decided to go downstairs to make tea for my mother's tray and get some breakfast."

"Was that your normal routine?" asked Wilson.

"Oh yes, Sergeant. I would always get up and make my mother a tray of tea, toast, marmalade. I would take that up to her before having anything myself. I suppose I don't need to do that anymore, do I?"

Peake made some notes on his pad.

"So, you walked down the stairs, Miss. Did you at anytime notice anything wrong, or out of place?"

"No. Nothing at all, not until I walked into the kitchen, and… found…" Sheila's voice petered out.

"When you found your mother, what did you do?" asked Wilson.

"I panicked, of course." There was a slightly acid note in Sheila's tone, and Peake -without remarking on it - made another note on his pad.

"That's quite understandable, Miss," agreed Sergeant Wilson. "What did you do when you panicked?"

"I cried, a lot, Sergeant. You can understand that, can't you?"

"Of course, Miss. Then, you did what?"

"Then I knew that I needed help. So, I rang Mister Jones, my next door neighbour. I hoped that he would know what to do, and he did."

"Yes, Mister Jones rang us, and we attended as quickly as possible."

"I am afraid I was too upset to notice, Sergeant."

"Miss Balsam, what can you tell us about your mother?"

"I don't understand."

"Were you aware of anyone she had upset, or had an argument with recently?"

"Besides me, sergeant?" Sheila put her hand to her mouth. "Oh, I shouldn't really say that, should I?"

"Don't worry, Miss Balsam. But yes, as well as you."

"Not really, you see she didn't have many friends, and rarely went out. We don't get many visitors so she doesn't see many people."

Inspector Peake made another note. "Miss Balsam," he said, speaking for the first time, "what can you tell us about what things were like between you and your mother? Had you had any reason to argue?"

"Not at all. We always get on very well."

"So there was no friction between you?"

"Of course there isn't!"

Peake made a note on his pad and nodded at Wilson.

"We saw…" Wilson shuffled some papers in his file… "some soil or compost spilt in the hallway?"

"Oh that was just a silly accident. I was moving a pot of lavender to make room for the unicorn statuette I've bought, and knocked it over."

"The unicorn?"

"The plant pot." Sheila's face puckered up, and she began to weep again. "I bought it for my mother for Mothers Day a few years ago. Now they are both gone."

"Both?" queried Wilson.

"My mother and the plant."

"Right, I see. So, Miss Balsam, how do you think an intruder got in?"

"I don't understand."

"Well, your mother has been attacked, so someone got into your house, didn't they?"

"Oh."

"So how do you think that they got into your house?" asked Peake.

"I don't know, I didn't think to look round. I just saw my mother lying there and couldn't think of anything else."

"Does anyone else have a key to the house? A relative? A neighbour?"

"No, my mother wouldn't allow that."

"There was no sign of a break in."

Sheila made no reply, but started to cry. Wilson looked at Peake. Peake returned the glance and nodded.

"I think that we'll leave it there for today, Miss Balsam."

"What happens now?"

"We will get someone to take you home," said Wilson. "I am afraid that we will have to ask you to carry out a difficult task tomorrow."

"What is that?" asked Sheila, still crying into a tissue.

"We will have to ask you to formally identify your mother's body, I'm afraid. Unless you have a close relative who can do that instead?"

"No, I'm sorry, there's no one else. I'll have to do it."

"When we take you home, is there a friend or a relative who could come and stay with you? Or would you like to go to a friend's house instead?"

Sheila didn't look up. "I'll be all right. If I need anything, then I'm sure that my neighbours can help me."

Wilson coughed, mildly embarrassed. "Miss Balsam, I'm afraid that your house will be, well..."

"You mean it won't be pleasant going back into my house, don't you sergeant?"

"Well, yes, miss."

"I've got to face up to it sometime. Sooner is better than later, isn't it?"

"I think that's very sensible, Miss Balsam," said Inspector Peake. "Thank you for being so helpful."

Peake stood up and beckoned to Wilson. "We'll arrange for you to be driven home, Miss Balsam," he said.

"Thank you, Inspector."

Sergeant Wilson tidied up the papers on the desk and put them back into the file. He stopped the tapes and labelled them. One he gave to Sheila, one he placed in a bag and added to the file.

"What's this for?" asked Sheila.

"Just for you, as a record. It's a procedure, Miss Balsam."

"Oh."

"Once again, I'm really sorry for your loss, Miss Balsam," said Peake. Followed by Wilson, Peake walked out of the interview room.

Sergeant Wilson followed Peake into Peake's office, and sat

down in the visitor's chair. Peake walked behind his desk and after sitting down, he opened his file and looked at his note pad.

"OK, Wilson, what do you think?"

"Of her?"

"Yes. Miss Balsam. What do you think?"

"Open mind, sir. She's not entirely consistent, is she? Sometimes she talks about her mother in the past tense, sometimes in the present tense."

"Her mother was just killed. I suppose we can't put anything on that."

"She dodged the question about a family argument, too, if you noticed, sir."

"I noticed," agreed Peake, napping his notepad.

"Then, there's her. I could understand if she was just upset all the time. I could understand if the shock left her cold to events. Numb. But one moment she sounds like a fluffy bunny that's been kicked, and the next, well, she seems much harder somehow."

"Too soon to take her off the list of suspects, then," said Peake.

"Especially as she's the only one on it. Locked house, no sign of forced or any other sort of entry: inside job has to be top of the list, doesn't it?"

"Motive?"

Wilson shrugged. "Family row. Anything like that. But at the moment she is the only one with the opportunity."

"Well, the post mortem will be a couple of days. Did the search team find a weapon?"

"Not so far. We still don't know what it was that did kill her, so they don't know what they are looking for, anyway."

"Let's just start with what we've got so far, and then decide what we do next," concluded Peake.

Chapter Four

I let myself into my house, and closed the front door with a sense of relief. I had developed an antipathy to being interviewed by policemen, and the experience had left me unhappy and unbalanced. And of course, having to see the dead body of my next door neighbour had made me feel rather ill. I made myself a cup of tea that was somewhat more refreshing than the tea I had been offered in the police station, took it through into my lounge and sat down. Half way through the cup, I leant back in my chair, and fell asleep.

I was woken some time later by a ferocious hammering on my front door. Alarmed, I hurried to the door before it sustained serious damage.

"Sheila!" I exclaimed, surprised.

"Oh, Mister Jones, can I come in?"

Sheila almost pushed past me and walked into my living room. By the time I had followed her there, she had fallen onto my sofa, and looked to be in a state of near collapse. As ever, when confronted by a damsel in distress, I panicked.

"Can I get you some tea?" I asked.

Sheila looked at me. "It's such a British thing, isn't it? Girl has her mother killed, make some tea. Girl is accused by the police of murdering her own mother, make some tea. Girl comes home to see that the police have turned her house upside down and made the most awful mess in every room, make some tea."

I looked at her, alarmed. "Have they accused you of killing your mother?"

"Well, maybe not. But it felt like it. And the mess! There's powder everywhere, the whole house looks like it has been ransacked. I just can't face it."

"Tea." I walked out of the living room and into the kitchen. Sheila followed me. I refilled the kettle and turned it on.

"I don't think I've been in your house before, Mister Jones."

"No, well, we don't know each other very well, do we?"

"I suppose not. It looks very like ours - like mine, I suppose it is now."

I looked around my kitchen. "From what I remember, you have better kitchen units than I do."

"Yes, mother insisted on new units when we bought the house. Because she spent a lot of time in the kitchen, that mattered to her."

I looked at Sheila carefully. Only this morning her mother had been killed, quite comprehensively, in their kitchen. The few times I had met Sheila, she had seemed to be quite dominated by her mother, and rather timid. I had expected to see her wailing her grief and loss, and was taken aback by the change to apparent composure from her very real grief just moments before. Perhaps she realised what I was thinking, for she suddenly gave a brittle-sounding laugh.

"I suppose that you were expecting me to be a wailing mess, Mister Jones?"

"Well, I don't know you very well, but it seems to me that you have every right to be very upset at this moment."

"Oh, I am, I am, I assure you. The kettle has boiled: might we have that tea?"

She must have caught my expression, for she laughed again. A strange sound in the circumstances. "Mister Jones, I am really not a homicidal maniac. Please, I really would like the tea. No sugar."

She turned and walked out of the kitchen, and back into my living room. After preparing the tea, I carried two large mugs into the living room and found her standing in front of the mirror I have on one wall, examining her reflection critically.

"Black will suit me," she said without turning round.

"Black suits everyone," I replied, putting down her tea on a side table.

Sheila turned away from the mirror and after picking up the mug of tea she sat down on a chair. "I'm afraid I'm going to ask you for another small favour, Mister Jones."

"Yes?"

"Oh I'm so grateful to you already for this morning, I hardly like to ask. But would you come round with me whilst I have a proper look around in the house, and see what needs doing?"

I sighed, but felt that I could hardly refuse.

"Good," Sheila said in a satisfied tone. She quickly finished her tea and stood up.

"Now?" I asked.

"There's no time like the present, my mother always told me. Tells me. Told me."

"Right now?" I asked.

"Please. Let's get it done." With a sudden shift of tone, the Sheila I knew returned. "I...I...I don't want to go back in there on my own, Mister Jones."

I was surprised by this, as I knew from what she had said to me that she had already been back into the house next door. But I put my tea onto the side table and followed her down the hall and out through the front door. With no sign of hesitancy, Sheila walked across my garden, and vaulted over the low fence between out properties. With mixed feelings I copied her. At her front door, she looked over her shoulder at me, her face half in shadow in the failing light.

"When you see inside, you'll understand why I wanted some company," she said to me. Then she unlocked the door and walked inside. I followed her into the hall.

Immediately I was surprised by the mess. Fingerprint powder in three different colours was blown about many surfaces, particularly around the front door itself and the large window in the hall. Directly below the window clear traces of soil were scattered wildly across the floor. Opposite the window was a stand, with a large terracotta statuette which seemed clear of any debris.

"This is not the worst," Sheila said, and walked down to the kitchen. I followed her to the doorway, and looked in amazement through the door. Again, the powders covered all the surfaces, some dried bloodstains were appallingly evident - as were the splinters and gouges in the woodwork of one of the kitchen units, and somewhat embarrassingly, the pile of stale vomit I recognised only too clearly as my own. I turned away, and looked into the living room. The efforts of the police search teams were only too evident.

"Sheila, is the upstairs…?"

"It's just the same, Mister Jones."

"Look, " I said reluctantly, "you can't stay here overnight. Have you a close friend that could put you up?"

"No, no I haven't. I was going to ask if you had a guest room I could use tonight?"

"Me?"

"It would be only one night, Mister Jones."

"But what…?"

"What would the neighbours say?" Sheila gave a brittle laugh. "They would be more likely to think you were in danger of being murdered by me!"

I didn't know what to say to that.

"I've already called a cleaning service. One of their people will do the hall, kitchen and living room tonight. I can deal with the upstairs, that's just untidy. And I've never really been the tidiest person. It drove my mother mad. Now I can be as untidy as I like!"

"Well of course I cannot refuse to help you, Sheila."

"Right. I pay for my board by ordering us a take away. Indian OK?"

She turned and walked out of the living room. I looked after her, rather bewildered, and more than a little concerned. I had no real experience, other than mine own, of grief and so supposed that it took people differently. I could hear voices at the front door, and walked into the hall to see who was there. Outside the front door, I could hear Sheila talking to someone I presumed was the cleaner. Looking around I saw the statuette and walked up to it for a closer look.

The statuette was made of what seemed to be a sort of pale terracotta, and represented a rearing unicorn. The horn resolutely faced the front door, as if to repel unwanted visitors. It had failed spectacularly, I reflected, for an unwanted visitor had found Mrs Balsam. I blinked, and it seemed as if the statuette trembled under my gaze. Oddly it did not seem old to look at, yet a sense of age radiated from it. Not only age, I came to realise as I studied the statuette. I gained a sense, a strong sense, of hostility and rage emanating from the statuette. I had been about to touch it, but that feeling was so strong that I drew back.

"Where did you get this?" I asked, not really knowing where Sheila was at that moment.

"My unicorn? Oh it was in a shop. I saw it and just fell in love with it at once," replied Sheila from outside the front door.

I looked at my hand. One finger had been scratched, and a small trace of blood could be seen across the fingerprint, yet I would have sworn that I never actually touched the unicorn.

Sheila opened the front door wide and beckoned to me. "Mister Jones, we need to let this lady from the agency get on with her work."

"Of course," I agreed. I looked again at the unicorn, and shook my head. "Sheila, do you not need clothes and stuff? If you are going to stay at mine tonight?"

Sheila laughed, an odd sound in that quiet house. "Of course. I'll only be a moment." She swept past me, her hand lovingly caressing the unicorn as she went. Then she walked upstairs, leaving me with the lady from the cleaning agency.

"They made a lot of mess, the police," she said.

"Yes, yes, I suppose they did." She had an accent I could not place, but I thought it impolite to ask.

"Poor lady, I am not surprised she is not wanting to stop here overnight." The cleaner smiled cheerfully. "I will make it all nice for her!"

"Have you seen the kitchen?" I could not help asking.

"Ooooh, is that where the murder happened?" asked the cleaner with relish. "Yes, yes, I would like to see that, please!"

"This way." I led the way down the hall, but chose not to enter the kitchen. The cleaner bustled in without hesitation.

"This room, this room too is a mess!" she exclaimed. "The police, they should have cleared all of this up for the poor lady. So here, here is where it happened?"

The daylight was fading, and I turned on the light in the hall. I also reached inside the kitchen, and pressed the light switch. Nothing happened. My shadow -was it my shadow?- from the hall ran across the floor of the kitchen and up the side of the gouged and damaged kitchen unit. The cleaner gave a delicious shiver and looked around happily. The contrast between the embers of the daylight filtering through the window and the harsh light from the hall made the kitchen seen unnatural and unsettling, especially in light of the recent event. The cleaner was entirely unaffected and appeared to me to be delighted to be somewhere so notorious. I shook my head in despair at human nature, and my shadow shifted with the movement. Then it seemed to change shape and grow, and I stepped back uneasily.

"Mister Jones!" said Sheila from behind me. I jumped in surprise, and realised that the changing shadow shape had simply been reflecting Sheila's unnoticed return downstairs. "You nearly trod on my foot!" she told me.

"Sorry."

"Right, I've packed an overnight bag." She looked into the kitchen, and seemed unaffected by the scene. "Maria," she addressed the cleaner, "do you need anything?"

"No, lady. I'm fine here. I have all the cleaning things I need in my car."

"Good. Mister Jones, perhaps we should let Maria here get on with her work." Sheila swung her overnight bag, and walked out of her house. I looked at Maria, who gave me a wide smile.

"Will you be all right?" I asked her.

"Sure, why ever not? Please, now I will start."

Maria turned to the kitchen sink, rooted about in the cupboard below and then started to fill a mop bucket with hot water. I shrugged, and left her to it.

"We are next door if you need anything," I reminded her as I walked away from the kitchen door.

"Sure, sure." She waved a dismissive hand at me without looking away from the rising water in the bucket.

*

Steam rose from the rising hot water in the mop bucket, and Maria nodded to herself in satisfaction. She turned off the tap, and with only a small grunt of effort lifted the mop bucket from the sink and put it down on the kitchen floor. A small amount of hot water slopped over the side onto the tiles, but she ignored that. Maria opened several of the kitchen cupboards. Each was inspected with a dissatisfied grunt.

"No bleach. No bleach. No bleach in a kitchen. Who has a kitchen and has no bleach? How I clean all this with no bleach? Not possible," she grumbled to herself. "Now Maria has to walk all the way back to her car for things."

Maria stood upright, and still grumbling under her breath used both her hands to ease her back. She suffered more and more from lower back pain, which the demands of her job exacerbated. She glared around the kitchen. "This light is poor, even with the lights on, the light is poor. Poor Maria must strain her eyes now, too," she muttered. Still, she had a collection of cleaning materials in her car, so she walked out of the kitchen into the hall. For a moment, she was startled, thinking that a shadow moved on the wall, but then she relaxed.

"All this mess, but they didn't touch the unicorn, the pigs," she said aloud. Stopping by the statuette, she placed one hand on her hip, and regarded the unicorn. Then she put a hand to her forehead, and splayed the fingers forward, making a horn, pointing her fingers at the front door and aping the unicorn's stance, as far as she was able. She leant backwards, wincing slightly, then laughed loudly and raucously. The unicorn trembled slightly at the sound. Maria opened the front door, and trudged down the path. Her car was parked at the end of the drive, and she huffed and panted along until she reached it. The boot was unlocked, and she opened it to reveal a carefully laid out box of cleaning materials. She selected the bleach, and as an after thought also picked up some surface cleaner and anti bacterial bathroom cleaner. Then she shut the car boot, rather more loudly than was necessary, and started back towards the house.

Whistling - rather badly - the last pop song she had heard on the car radio, Maria frowned at the front door of the house. It had swung almost closed whilst she had walked to the car and back, so she shouldered the door of the house open, and stepped inside. The front door swung back closed behind her, and the latch clicked shut, locking the door. Maria ignored it as Sheila had given her a spare key.

She cocked her head to one side, and examined the statuette again. "Ha!" she exclaimed. "I thought you pointed other way, mister statue!" She shook her head, her hair swaying, and laughed at herself. Then she took the kitchen work surface cleaner and spayed a fine mist over the statuette. For a moment she thought about wiping the drops of cleaner from the pale unicorn, but then changed her mind. She reached out to pat the horn with her right hand.

Maria froze when she placed her hand on the statuette. Unbidden, long forgotten childhood memories rose and fell, before she suddenly recalled an incident with her brother for the first time in many years. Her brother had caught a cat, and was killing it very slowly and painfully in the field beyond their house. Drawn by the noise, Maria approached, and squatted down to watch. She remembered how she felt a thrill of excitement watching her brother cause pain and distress, and how vital and alive she had felt in contrast to the suffering caused to the stray cat. For years then she had felt ashamed of the memory, ashamed of her reaction, but suddenly now it seemed to be something to celebrate. For a long moment she was transported to a time and place where such things were commonplace and normal. Then the moment passed.

She shook her head, confused, and then recalled what she was doing. "Clean this maybe when I come back to do the door," she said. Then Maria walked down the hall and into the kitchen. She frowned, as even with the electric lighting the room was still dimly lit. Maria turned to the tall cupboard that stood beside the door, and opened it. She gasped in surprise as she realised that it was not a cupboard, but the entrance to a cellar with a very small landing, and a flight of extremely steep steps. She rocked unsteadily on her feet, and held tight to the door for balance.

"Stupid, stupid!" she gasped. "Stupid place for a door. Dangerous, those stairs." Dramatically, she clasped one hand over her heart and breathed heavily. The cellar door moved against her hand, and the mop hanging from a hook on the back of the door swung and banged sharply on the door. She jumped again, then seized the mop in her hand, and slammed the door shut. The vibration made the kitchen lights vibrate, and the shadows shifted uneasily. As did Maria.

"I getting old," she told herself. She shivered, and pulled her overall a little more closely around her frame.

Maria dropped the cleaning products on the worktop, and leant the mop against the nearest cupboard. Then, after a brief struggle with the child proof top to the bleach, she poured a large quantity of the cleaning fluid into the bucket. She plunged the mop into the bucket, several times, to thoroughly mix the water and bleach, and then applied the dripping mop to the remaining pool of dried blood on the floor. The dark brown stain turned a lighter colour, and as Maria industriously applied the mop the stain grew less as the water in the bucket began to turn first pink and then a deeper red, the low lighting adding a sombre tone to the water.

In the hall, beside the kitchen door, the flickering shadows started to thicken and coalesce.

Maria grunted as the mop struggled with a hardened bloodstain on the tiles and then grunted again in satisfaction as the stain finally surrendered to her efforts. She squeezed the mop out into the bucket, and put it to one side.

Dark upon the wall, the shadows began to grow upwards and the suspicion of a horn started to form at the very top of the otherwise indistinct shape.

Maria picked up the heavy mop bucket, using both hands. Unsteadily she carried it across to the sink, and with some relief emptied the foul smelling water and dried blood out of the bucket. The red tinged water swirled wildly in the sink as if agitated in some way. Maria turned and picked up the bottle of bleach. As the bloodied water slowly drained away she turned on the tap, rinsed out the sink and then poured some bleach down the drain. The odour of blood was replaced by the bright, fresh smell of the bleach.

In the hall, the darkening shadow halted and then slowly began to fade.

The sink emptied again, and Maria lifted the bucket back up, and positioned it under the tap. Whilst the bucket slowly refilled, she grabbed the bathroom cleaner and sprayed the agent all around the window and the back door, covering everywhere that had been touched by the fingerprint powder. As the water in the bucket reached the maximum level she could manage, she turned off the tap and lifted the bucket down, placing it close to the dried vomit. She poured more bleach into the bucket and then attended to the door again.

"Pigs, dirty pigs. Leaving house like this for lady. Not right, not right at all!" she complained loudly, and began wiping the powder away from the door frame. When she had finished, she opened more kitchen cupboards until she found some polish and a duster. She wiped industriously at the door, until even in the dim lighting it shone. "Why no proper lights?" she wondered. "Dark, so dark." Putting down the cloth, she sprayed cleaner all around the window frame again, as the earlier cleaner had dried. Then she wiped hard at the powder with some kitchen roll, putting each piece into the waste bin as it became too damp.

Slowly, so slowly, the window cleared of dust. Maria put down the cleaner and cloth and reached for the polish and duster. She liberally sprayed polish over the window, and replaced the aerosol. Lifting the duster, she wiped the window and jumped back in surprise at a sudden and unexpected reflection in the glass.

"Hahaha," she laughed at herself. "I must be jumpy tonight. For a moment I thought I saw that unicorn-ey thing from the hall."

She finished wiping down the window and her own face stared back at her, still smiling. Maria put the cloth down, and picked up the mop. She dunked it into the bucket of clean water and bleach, and rinsed the mop out. In the bucket, the water turned pink again. Maria applied the mop to the kitchen floor, and cleaned the whole area, smiling to herself in satisfaction. The floral, lavender, scent of the bleach filled the kitchen, and even the lights seemed a little brighter.

Maria scrubbed busily then at the kitchen worktops, tut-tutting away to herself at the state of them. "Now," she said aloud again, "now I must do the front door. And I will vacuum the hall, too!" Sheila had thoughtfully left the vacuum cleaner out in the living room, so Maria left the kitchen and walked across the hall towards the living room door. As she did so, she shivered.

"Is cold in here," she complained. "Must be window left open somewhere. Now, should I turn on the heating so that lady is warm when she comes in? No. It is a waste, a waste of lady's money. She is stopping next door tonight with the nice gentleman there, so does not need house heated tonight. More than stopping, perhaps? Eh?" she shook her head. "No, no. He too old for her, I think. Lady is young, and wants young man, that for sure. Not middle-aged like him. Wonder why he not married? Maybe he want me? No? No. Ah well."

Wincing at her back pain, Maria knelt down and plugged in the vacuum cleaner. She switched it on, and pushed it out of the living room, and down the hall. Carefully she cleaned up the spilt soil, and then ran the cleaner backwards and forward, making sure that she cleaned to the very edges of the carpet. The unicorn statuette wobbled slightly, and she put out her hand and steadied it on its stand.

The front door was also covered in the fingerprint powder. Maria scowled at it. It would need a lot of cleaning. She walked back down the hall towards the brighter light of the kitchen and the clean lavender scent from the bleach. But almost at the door, she stopped.

"Hey! Hey, you! What you do in here?" she demanded. "You no right to be in here!"

Just in front of her, half hidden to her vision in the dim light of the hall but his shadow sharply defined by the kitchen lights, a man stood with his back to her. He did not speak. Maria backed away, frightened by his silence and his stillness.

"You! Man! You leave, you leave now. How you got in, you go out. Go! Go now!"

Although Maria thought that he was facing away from her, the man stepped towards her, and she realised with horror that he seemed to be made from the shadows. He had no clothes, he needed no clothes. The shadows that formed his shape both revealed and concealed him. He had no discernable face but his glowing red eyes shone clearly. His mouth smiled and she could see the gleam of his teeth. Then, growing from the middle of his forehead she could see a horn.

Maria scrabbled frantically for her rosary and the crucifix attached to the cord. Her mouth opened, and she tried to call out for help: but no sound came in that quiet, still house. Maria tried to scramble back to escape, but the shadowman was too close. Terror, sheer terror overwhelmed her. The malevolence and hunger that drove him flooded out and poured over her. His arms reached out, the fingers of his hands sharply defined and sharply tipped with long nails. His hands closed behind her. The grip of the hands behind her on her shoulders was insistent and Maria at last found her voice to scream and scream and scream as the shadowman enveloped her and the darkness enfolded her and took her deep within itself.

The red eyes shone brightly, the horn gleamed golden and black in the dusk of the hall, and Maria slumped to the floor. Her rosary fell to one side from her limp hand and the shadows drew back a little to avoid its touch. Without needing to turn, the shadowman paced slowly towards the kitchen, dragging Maria's body behind him. At the door he paused slightly as if in discomfort, but with strength of purpose he passed into the clean kitchen. Only a few moments later, the kitchen light went out. In the dim light cast by the failing hall light, the shadows thickened about the kitchen door, darkened, then faded.

The house was again empty.

Or perhaps not.

Chapter Five

Sheila turned over uncomfortably in the strange bed. Sleeping uneasily, she kicked at the sheets with her feet and made a more comfortable space for them. The mattress had the feel of a bed that was largely unused. The sheets were clean and aired but clearly the spare room in Mister Jones' house received few guests. The room was polished - which surprised her a little - and very blandly furnished in neutral colours, which did not. Her clothes lay scattered on the floor, her overnight bag dropped carelessly below the window.

She awoke, and realised that she had not taken off her wristwatch. Sitting up, she was surprised to see one of her cuddly toys and then realised that she had packed it with her plum coloured pyjamas when she had hastily prepared the overnight bag.

A box of tissues lay on the pillow beside her, and several used tissues lay on top of the duvet. With a start she remembered that she had cried herself to sleep. With another start she suddenly recalled that for a long part of the day she had not in fact felt sadness for the brutal killing of her mother, and she started to cry again with heavy, racking but silent sobs. Sheila wondered for a moment why she kept so quiet in her grief, but then realised that instinctively she knew that Mister Jones was too kind to allow her to sob noisily without in someway trying to offer her comfort and that she really did not want that.

Outside, the world was dark, the moon closed away by heavy clouds. The wind rose and lying awake in the strange bed Sheila felt uneasy and insecure. The curtains were not fully closed and she could see the orange glow of the street light filtering in through the gap. It felt oddly warm and comforting, and she turned over and slipped down below the duvet. Then she pushed her arm out from underneath the covers, and twisted it until the faint glow reflected onto the face of her wristwatch. She squinted until she could make out the time. It was after two in the morning. Sheila sighed heavily: at least another four hours before she could get up: the downside of being in someone else's home. She dragged her arm back under the duvet, and shivered.

Closing her eyes, Sheila tried not to think of what the cleaner had been doing next door. "How could I have felt so detached?" she wondered. "Shock, I suppose," she said aloud in an attempt to convince herself that all her reactions and actions had been logical and explainable. To convince herself that her behaviour and feelings had been normal reactions to the grief she expected to feel.

The wind rose, and the sound of the guttering moving under the onslaught first frightened and then soothed her. It was a natural, normal sound on an unnatural night. A light patter of rain beat against the window, and when the rain stopped there came a single knock, as she drifted back into a light sleep. Sheila awoke again and lay silent and still in the bed.

The knock was repeated.

Sheila frowned. Mister Jones was several years older than her: and in any case she had never thought for a moment that he would try to take advantage of her, or she would not have sought his spare room. Or would she? That was an intriguing thought for her, and she ignored the third knock as she examined it. In her almost dream she came to no conclusion.

The fourth knock brought her fully awake, although it was still muffled and soft.

"If that is Mister Jones, why does he not open the door?" she asked herself. "If he wants to check on me, he could... or if he wants something else, then surely he would... and what would I want?"

She listened hard, as the next knock sounded out above the rattle of the plastic guttering in the wind, still soft but somehow more insistent.

"The heating pipes probably," she said to herself and rolled over to face away from the door. Facing away from the door in Mister Jones' spare room meant that she was now lying on her side, looking towards the wall. From behind her, she heard a door open softly. For a moment she froze as she heard soft footsteps, but then she realised that she could hear Mister Jones walking along the landing outside the bedroom. She listened as he opened the door to the bathroom, and a minute or two later she heard the toilet flush. Still rigid in the spare bed, tense and focussed on every sound other than the wind outside the house, she heard the sound of the bathroom door close.

Mister Jones padded quietly past the door, and she listened as he closed the door to his own room that lay beside the spare room. Clearly he was making an effort not to disturb her, and she relaxed.

Then came the next knock, louder and clearly not on the door but on the wall. The orange glow from the streetlight flickered as the lamp post swayed in the strong wind. A further knock seemed more insistent, and Sheila tensed again. Whatever was Mister Jones playing at? She sat up and swung her legs out of bed, and as she did so she realised that the repeated knocking was not in fact coming from the wall to Mister Jones' bedroom, but from the wall that separated his house from hers.

Sheila chilled at the thought. The wind howled around the house, which seemed to shake under the onslaught, but still she heard the soft but insistent knock on the wall. "It's the cleaner, of course," she told herself in relief. "She'll be busy upstairs. And next to this room, well that's my room in our house so..."

Sheila felt much happier, and rolled back onto the bed under the covers. Turning onto her back she lay back and closed her eyes again.

The next knock on the wall was accompanied by a breath of sound, and her eyes opened widely. She stared at the bland, oatmeal coloured ceiling and tried very hard indeed not to feel scared. She strained to hear - to not hear - the next noise. Not a knock this time, it was as if a nail ran down a sheet of glass, a chalk on a blackboard, a fingernail on her spine: a long, soft and eldritch scratch on the wall, accompanied by a moan on the edge of her hearing. The moan seemed to call her name and Sheila dived under the covers.

The window rattled, and her name came a little more loudly, as if carried by the wind. The scratch on the far side of the wall was repeated more urgently. Sheila put her hands over her ears and pressed them tight, her heart rate rising. The window rattled again, more urgently and Sheila threw the covers to one side in a sudden motion and stood upright beside the bed. In one stride she reached the window, threw the curtains aside and stared out into the night.

The streetlight still swayed in the wind, and the shadows cast by the trees swayed and waved across the gardens below the window. Urgently she looked at the street, and looked from side to side: other than the windswept trees all was still. The orange sodium street light glinted on the roofs of the parked cars. The garden gates threw their fixed and immobile shadows down the paths towards the front doors below this window.

Sheila sighed and reached up with both hands to grasp the now open curtains. As she did so, the scratching noise was repeated loudly and insistently from directly outside the window. She stepped back in alarm, then strode back and fearfully peered outside. On the grass below the window there was a motionless shadow. It seemed to resemble a figure, with a horn growing from the head. The rain again beat against the window directly in front of her face and startled, she jumped backwards.

"My unicorn!" breathed Sheila. As she spoke, the noise came again and the shadow on the grass twisted, and with a gasp of relief Sheila realised that the noise was caused by the branches of a wisteria plant that grew up the wall and surrounded the window. Not by some supernatural agency, as she had begun to fear. The wind moaned again, Sheila moaned in relief along with the wind, and the shadow on the grass trembled a little. The branch scraped on the wall outside the window.

"How stupid am I!" said Sheila softly to herself. "How silly do you have to be to start thinking such daft things!"

After checking that the window was tightly shut, she pulled the curtains against the wind and rain and turned back to the bed. A shadow had lain across the bed, cast by the street light, and as she moved away from the window and the closed curtains the shadow faded away.

Sheila giggled at herself, bounced happily onto the bed and tossed the duvet around until it covered her completely. She giggled again and snuggled down under the covers and composed herself to drift happily back to sleep. The next scratch on the wall was accompanied by an unmistakeable calling of her name and terrified her completely.

"Who is it?" she said, her voice muffled by the duvet covering her head.

"Sheila," called the voice again, more distinctly. It was a male voice, cultured, adult, somehow old.

"Who is it? Who are you?" asked Sheila more loudly.

The scratching came insistently on the wall between the two houses. "Sheila, Sheila…" called the voice. To Sheila the voice felt like dark, bitter chocolate might sound and she shivered deep inside, as something in her nature responded.

"Who are you? What do you want?" cried Sheila.

"Sheila, Sheila…" called the voice again.

"Sheila?" there was a loud knock on the bedroom door, and with a start Sheila recognised Mister Jones' voice. "Sheila? Are you all right? Do you need anything?"

"Mister Jones?" Sheila replied.

Jones must have interpreted that as a form of invitation, for he opened the door slightly and without either entering the room or even looking inside he asked: "Sheila? Are you all right? Only I thought that I heard you call out and I was concerned for you." The landing light was on, and his shadow ran across the floor of the room ahead of him. Sheila shuddered.

"Thank you, thank you," replied Sheila. "Possibly I did call out, but that is because I think that I had a bad dream."

"Well, that I can understand," replied Mister Jones. "You have had an awful day, a day I cannot begin to contemplate. Can I get you anything? I don't have any sleeping tablets, I'm afraid, just some paracetemol."

"No, no, I'm fine. Honestly, I'm fine. I really, really appreciate your concern. But I'm fine."

"Well, if you are sure," said Mister Jones, sounding to Sheila very unconvinced.

"Yes, yes. As well as I can be, anyway."

"Call me if you need anything."

Mister Jones shut the door, hiding the light from the landing, and the room returned to darkness. Sheila lay rigid in the bed, fearful to sleep and fearful to remain awake.

"Please let daybreak come soon," she prayed - to whom she knew not.

Sheila lay in the bed, tense and agitated, waiting for the next noise, the next sound, the next use of her name. Only silence was her reward, and she finally drifted into sleep. Her sleep became so deep that the gentle knocking on the wall did not arouse her. Outside the wind and rain reached a crescendo, a tempest, a tumult: and still Sheila slept. Finally the storm died although the world outside was ominously dark.

The scratching gradually became more and more insistent. A small piece of plaster slipped from the centre of the wall and fell slowly to the floor. Sheila grunted in her sleep and turned onto her side, facing the wall. Motes of dust spiralled downwards, followed by another small piece of plaster. There was silence, then again Sheila's name was called, softly but insistently.

Sheila stirred. A crack appeared in the wall and more plaster fell. Sheila moaned, and shifted uneasily. More dust drifted from the wall, and finally a small hole appeared. Even in the dark room, the hole appeared to be jet black. Darkness flowed slowly through the hole, drifted like the dust, hung in the air. Then slowly it coalesced upon the wall and collected, gathered, and grew. Rising up along the bedroom wall against the cream plaster, it formed slowly the shape of a man: a tall man, with a single horn growing from his forehead.

Sheila opened her eyes, and froze. Slowly she cast the covers to one side and sat upright. Then she turned to her right and lowered her feet to the floor of the bedroom, feeling the soft tufts of the carpet between her toes. She raised her eyes to the shadow shaped head, and stopped. Slowly a red gleam appeared on either side of the shadow head, and widened. Finally two glowing red eyes regarded Sheila. Their expression was unreadable, but their glow deepened and spread out until Sheila was bathed in their light.

The shadowman stepped forward, away from the wall, and held

out his hands. Sheila slowly stood up, her eyes locked on the glowing red eyes in the face that hung above her. The horn dipped towards her as his face tilted towards hers.

The shadow man held out his hands to her in a welcoming, unthreatening gesture. Responding, Sheila reached out and took the shadow hands in hers. Darkness flowed over and around them, enfolding her willing hands and then slowly spreading to her wrists and slipping up her arms. Beyond the curtains, in the world outside, the first rays of dawn broke over the horizon flooding the world with promise and daylight as Sheila held and embraced the darkness before her.

*

The night had been stormy and the rain lashing my bedroom window, driven by the wild wind, had woken me several times. Of course, starting the day by finding my next door neighbour horribly killed in her own kitchen would never have been the precursor to the most peaceful night for me, but the distraction of the bad weather was just too much. I was just contemplating giving up on sleep and had reached for my book when a slight noise made me pause. My finger was already on the switch for the bedside light, and I pressed it harder than was necessary. I had already sat upright, otherwise I would have jerked upwards. The noise came again.

"Mice?" I asked myself. I listened intently as the sound was repeated. Then I realised that the sound was being carried through the plaster wall of my room, and in fact the sound was from the spare room in which my guest lay, hopefully asleep.

"If it is mice, I hope they don't wake her," I thought. "The poor girl has had more than enough to contend with for one day. Finding her mother murdered like that must have been awful for her. The shock can't have hit her yet."

The scratching noise echoed a little more loudly, and I frowned. "If they carry on, they will wake her - if she's asleep. I'll have to get some poison and put it down for them tomorrow."

Satisfied rather than cheered by that thought, I threw the covers to one side and decided to visit the toilet. Slightly embarrassed at doing so with a visitor in the house - for I am unused to house guests - I walked as quietly as I could down out of my bedroom, and down the landing to the bathroom. No light gleamed under the door to the spare bedroom, and I hoped that Sheila was in fact sleeping, even though the noise of the storm was rising.

I visited the bathroom, flushed the toilet and walked as softly as I could back to my own bedroom, and closed the door behind me. My bed had, I found, cooled down rapidly in my absence, and with a muffled curse I turned off the light and pulled the covers over my head. But that failed to mask the repeated scratching, and then - softly and indistinct, I heard a voice.

"A bad dream. She'll be having a bad dream," I said to myself and rolled over. Then I heard, faint but distinct, another voice. This seemed to be calling her name and there was something about that voice that made all the hairs on the back of my neck rise. Although I could not hear the words, I heard Sheila respond.

"Is she using her mobile phone?" I said, aloud this time. How could I know? I was reluctant to disturb her. What would she think? In a near stranger's home and disturbed by him in the small hours of the morning? Her voice was a little louder whilst still indistinct, and the other voice I could hear: it felt awfully wrong, and for a moment I was afraid that such a voice could even be heard within my home. Then I heard Sheila's voice clearly and distinctly.

"Who are you? What do you want?" she demanded, quite loudly.

That was enough. Again I threw off the covers, and turned on my light. Opening my bedroom door, I turned on the landing light too, and took the four paces to the door of my spare bedroom. I knocked on the door, and called her name.

"Sheila? Sheila? Are you all right? Do you need anything?" I asked. I was hesitant to open the door, but the other voice: a male voice I now realised was still. Was she alone?

"Mister Jones?" Sheila asked.

"Sheila? Are you all right? Only I thought that I heard you call out and I was concerned for you." I opened the door, just a little but did not enter the room. The landing light ran into the bedroom, and I could see the lower half of the bed through the partly opened door. The covers were disturbed, but clearly did not hide another person.

"Thank you, thank you," replied Sheila. "Possibly I did call out, but that is because I think that I had a bad dream."

"Well, that I can understand," I told her. "You have had an awful day, a day I cannot begin to contemplate. Can I get you anything? I don't have any sleeping tablets, I'm afraid, just some paracetemol."

"No, no, I'm fine. Honestly, I'm fine. I really, really appreciate your concern. But I'm fine."

"Well, if you are sure," I said. I was still perturbed by the other voice, but unwilling to walk uninvited into a bedroom - even though it was my spare bedroom - occupied by a solitary and vunerable young woman.

"Yes, yes. As well as I can be, anyway."

"Call me if you need anything."

There seemed to be little else that I could do at that point, and so I closed her door. I returned to the door of my room, turned off the landing light and shut the bedroom door. I stood on the landing in the darkness, not entirely sure what I was doing. I was obviously intruding on her privacy by listening to a private conversation, and felt very awkward about that: yet at the same time as her host I had some responsibility for her safety if this male - and somehow repellent and disturbing - voice represented a threat to her.

I stood for some minutes on the dark landing whilst the storm outside became progressively more violent. The house shook under the more violent gusts, and I started to feel very cold. Clearly I was doing nothing useful, and so I opened my bedroom door, only half closed it behind me and went back to bed. Finally I fell asleep, but was troubled by dark and disturbing dreams.

I awoke finally to full daylight. The storm had blown itself out in the night, or had passed on to wreak its violence on other unfortunates, and when I opened my curtains the world was still. My bedroom window overlooked my back garden, and I could see that one of the panels from the tall wooden fence that separated my garden from that of the house next door - Sheila's garden - had been rudely torn from the fence posts and hurled across the grass. It lay in shattered ruin on my lawn, and even at that distance I could see that it was clearly beyond repair.

Then to my surprise I saw Sheila. She was standing on my lawn close to the gap in the fence. Her hair looked wild as though it had not been brushed this morning, and although I did not know her well enough to know any of her personal habits, that seemed to me in my limited experience of women, a little unusual. She looked around my garden, then without looking back at my house or up at the window where I was standing, she stepped through the gap in the fence, and pushed through the bushes that were planted in a wide flowerbed on her side of the fence. With a start I realised that these were rose bushes, and wondered why she appeared unaffected by the thorns.

Quickly I dressed, and walked out of my bedroom onto the landing. The door to the guest room was closed, and I thought about opening it. With one hand on the door handle, I stopped. Sheila had not been carrying her case when I saw her in the garden, so it seemed as if she would return; in which case opening the door to the bedroom she had just vacated might be an unpardonable breach of her privacy. I turned away and walked down the stairs, and into the kitchen. The kettle was boiling, and two mugs were set out on the worktop, tea bags already in place. The normality of the scene was reassuring, and I stood beside the kettle. Should I follow Sheila across the garden?

I was saved from making a decision by her return. She walked in through the still open kitchen door, and smiled at me.

"Mister Jones! I thought I was going to have to wake you up with a cup of tea."

"Did you sleep all right, Sheila?" I asked, carefully.

"Yes, thank you. It must have been the storm that disturbed me, but after you checked on me - and thank you for that, by the way - I went off and slept like a log."

"I'm glad," I told her. "How are you this morning?"

"I'm fine, thank you. Why shouldn't I be? Oh, you mean my mother."

I thought that coming downstairs in a morning to find your mother killed rather horribly might have a more lasting effect on someone. But I thought it politic not to say so right then. After all, grief can take each of us differently, I thought. "Yes, your mother," I replied.

"Mister Jones, you have to understand. My mother, well she wasn't very nice. I know that you did not know either of us very well, after all we have not been neighbours for all that long, have we? But she was not the nicest person. I feel free now!"

"Free?" I asked.

"Free!" Sheila replied. She walked up to me and pushed me gently to one side before pouring the freshly boiled water onto the tea bags. She then took milk out of the fridge and poured some into one cup. "Milk?" she asked me.

I shook my head, and looked at her carefully. "You've been next door - to your house?" I asked.

"Yes. I wanted to check on the cleaner. She seems to have gone, and the kitchen is fine now. But the storm has damaged our fence, hasn't it?"

"I saw that from my window. I'll ring the insurance company and get a man out."

"Don't worry about that, Mister Jones. Anyway, I've slept in your home now, so we must be good enough friends not to worry if there is free access between our houses!"

Sheila laughed, and drank some tea, smiling at me over the rim of the mug.

I was actually beginning to feel a little concerned about Sheila. My parents had both died many years ago, and although we had not been close, we had not had a poor relationship either. I could recall their passing - peacefully as it happened and not long apart - and I had not responded in the way Sheila was now. She seemed detached and almost unconcerned about her loss, and in a small way I began to worry about her.

She seemed to sense my caution, for she clasped her mug with both hands and looked at me.

"Mister Jones, you must think that I am unfeeling, even uncaring. That is not the case."

I drank some of my tea and looked at her.

"To be honest, my mother was a tyrant, Mister Jones. She ordered me around, treated me as her personal servant and never had a kind word to say to me. She was my mother and I will miss her, but I am not so hypocritical as to pretend that I am not glad that she has gone."

"Even in that awful way?"

"Mister Jones, do you believe in karma?"

"Well, some days, perhaps."

"Can you believe that those who do evil bring evil down upon themselves?"

"Bad things happen to bad people?" I suggested.

"If you like."

"Yes, I can believe that, Sheila."

"Well, there you are then."

"My problem is that there are some evils that visit themselves on those of us who try to be good, as well. And evil tends to spread itself about without having too much regard for the consequences."

"You think I should be grieving, don't you, Mister Jones?"

"It might be healthier for you," I suggested, looking at her closely. She was standing close to me and I looked down into her eyes. The pupils were very dark.

"Play the dutiful daughter, you mean?" she snorted in derision and looked away.

"Sheila, your mother has been murdered. The police are going to be asking questions."

She snorted again. "That won't bring the old witch back to trouble me though, will it? And I didn't do it, so I have no need to worry about them. No, she is gone where they won't find her."

"Where is that?" I asked.

"Hades, Mister Jones. Hades. Where she belongs." Sheila put down her mug, having drained her tea. "I'll get my stuff now. Thank you for last night. Even though I am glad to see her gone, I don't think I could have slept there last night. Now that the cleaner has done her job though, I'm happy to be back there with my own things around me."

That I could understand, at least. Her attitude still worried me, but I began to wonder if I was simply taking an old fashioned attitude: and of course I had not been the victim of the sort of abusive relationship that Sheila was describing to me and maybe as a result I had no right to comment or to feel uneasy. Yet I still felt uneasy for her, and those dark pupils were still somehow disturbing.

Sheila walked past me into my hall, and I heard her climb my stairs. I finished my tea, and refilled the kettle to make some more. Before the kettle had boiled for the second time that morning, Sheila had returned downstairs carrying her overnight bag.

"Mister Jones, thank you for your hospitality. I intend to repay you for your kindness."

"Sheila, you have no need to do that."

"Oh, I absolutely insist! I feel that I owe you a debt, and such debts must always be repaid!" Sheila walked up to me, and unexpectedly stood on her toes and kissed me on the cheek. Her overnight bag banged against my leg, and she patted my arm in apology with her free hand. Then without another word she walked out of the kitchen door, and across the wet grass towards her own home.

I put my hand to my cheek, where she had kissed me. My cheek felt odd, quite cold. But I am unused to being kissed, and so paid that no attention. The kettle whistled cheerfully so I dropped a fresh teabag into the mug and filled it again with water. Leaving the tea to gather strength, I though I had better take the bedding from the spare room and wash it in case - unlikely as that might be - I had another visitor.

I left the kitchen and walked up the stairs to the landing. At the door to the spare room I paused. Last night there had been a terrific storm. Sheila had walked across two gardens, and back again; then she had climbed my stairs to this room without taking off her shoes. I looked down at the cream coloured carpet on the landing and on the stairs, expecting to see footmarks to be cleaned later in the day. There were none. Not a race of damp, of soil, or of mud marked the stair carpet. I opened the door to strip the bedding from the spare bed, and stopped, rooted to the spot. I stared at the wall between the houses, at the cracked and broken plaster, and the gaping hole through which I could see into the front bedroom of the house next door.

Chapter Six

Sheila walked across the wet grass with a firm and purposeful tread. She opened the kitchen door to her house, walked inside and then put her overnight bag on the kitchen table. She looked all around the kitchen, and then started to laugh, a high wild sound, with just a hint of hysteria.

"Mine! Mine now! All mine!" she shouted. Her voice echoed in the empty house. She closed the door to the garden behind her, and turned the key in the lock to secure the door. Then she stepped around the kitchen table, and with no discernable emotion regarded the still and lifeless body of Maria, the cleaner. "Whatever am I to do with you?" she asked. "You were a cleaner. I can't have you lying there looking untidy, can I?"

Sheila tilted her head to one side and thought. "I can't take you out of the front, can I? It's daylight. Someone will notice me. Bet Mister Jones would. Oh yes, I bet he would." She looked out of the kitchen window. "Can't plant her. I suppose those wretched policemen will come calling again, and convenient as it would be, they might notice a newly dug grave."

She tilted her head the other way, as if listening to a new idea.

"They didn't see the cellar, did they? They even asked me where it was, and I told them we didn't have one. She can go down there." Sheila looked at Maria's body, and then stepped over her. "She doesn't look very heavy. I'm sure that I am strong enough to move her."

She bent down and took hold of one lifeless arm. She tugged

hard, and the corpse shifted easily. Sheila laughed again. "Oh yes, I'm strong enough, aren't I? I was strong enough to shift mother about when she demanded it, so this one will present no problems. There's nothing left in her to complain at me!" Sheila knelt down beside the body, and looked at the lifeless face. "Why ever did you look so frightened? It can't have lasted long enough to hurt." She looked up, and looked at the deeply scored grooves on the cupboard door that marked the spot where her mother had died. "I hope she hurt though," she said vindictively. "I hope she screamed and screamed and screamed." Sheila paused. "Tell me she did..." she added. "Tell me that she howled all the way down." She tilted her head as if listening and smiled in a satisfied way.

Sheila stood up, using the kitchen table as a support. "Right, madam. Let's get you out of view before some nosey parker comes calling." She turned and opened the cupboard door that in fact led down to the cellar. She let go of the door, and it swung partly closed. For a moment, a spasm of anger crossed Sheila's face. Then it cleared, and she left the cupboard door. The mop bucket stood on the floor next to the sink, and Sheila dragged it across the floor to the cellar door. Pulling the door open again she used the mop bucket to prop it open, and turned back to Maria.

"Come on, you!" she said aloud. Stooping, Sheila grabbed Maria's body under each shoulder and straightened up. " Not much of you, is there?" she said. Slowly she stepped backwards, but then stopped on the landing at the top of the stairs.

"You first, Maria!" Sheila said cheerfully and swung the body around, panting for the first time from the exertion. She let go of Maria with her right hand, and fumbled for the light switch.

Finding the pull cord, she gave it a swift tug and the cellar light came on. The stone steps were quite steep and led down at an angle. Sheila positioned the body's feet at the top of the stairs and gave a shove. The body slid down the steps, and came to rest at the bottom of the stairs in an untidy heap.

Sheila made a satisfied noise and walked sedately down the stairs into the cellar. She jumped over the body onto the cellar floor, and looked around carefully. The floor of the cellar was of wide stone slabs, but completely free of clutter. One of the walls held some racking on which a selection of ordinary household tools was scattered. Against the opposite wall leant a long thin table, covered in dust.

"This will do very well," said Sheila, satisfied. Again she titled her head as if listening to a voice that only she could hear. One of Maria's shoes had fallen off in the descent from the kitchen. Sheila pulled the other shoe off, and cast it into a corner. She took hold of Maria's ankles, and dragged the body into the very centre of the cellar. Maria's skirt had rucked up to the top of her thighs, and Sheila pulled the body's ankles well apart, forcing the skirt still higher. She walked around, and placed each arm at ninety degrees from the body, to resemble the sketches of the human frame made by Da Vinci.

Then Sheila stood back and regarded the corpse. "I saw you look at him, Maria. You didn't think I did, but I saw you look at him. I don't think Mister Jones would be very interested in you now, would he? Look at your dumpy legs. Ladders in your stockings-o too. Cheap knickers. No, he wouldn't be interested in looking at anything else either, would he? Not now." She bent down, and one by one undid the buttons on Maria's blouse. She pulled the fabric apart, and smiled as she inspected the open pale wound below the heart. No blood seeped from the wound or stained the cold flesh. Maria's skirt had a long zipper that ran down the length of the skirt. Sheila tugged the skirt until the zip could run freely, and she unzipped the whole length of the skirt. She tugged at the fabric until it came free, and she threw the skirt across the cellar towards the table.

On the thin table lay a dusty kitchen knife and a long disused piece of yellow chalk. Sheila left the body, and picked up both. The knife she dropped between Maria's ankles: using the chalk she bent down and began to draw a circle around the body. The chalk scratched and squeaked on the cold stone floor, but she persisted until she had completed an entire circle. The chalk line enclosed the body tightly, almost touching the lifeless fingertips and cold feet. Sheila climbed several of the cellar steps and regarded the body in the inscribed circle carefully.

She smiled in satisfaction, and walked back down the steps. She returned the chalk to the table and picked up the knife from the floor. Bending forward, Sheila touched the tip of the knife to the heart wound. She took exaggerated care not to touch or mar the chalk circle at all. Slowly, lightly, almost lovingly and taking care not to mark the flesh she ran the tip of the knife down the body to the underclothes. Carefully she slipped the tip of the knife under the waistband and sliced through each side panel of the fabric before stopping abruptly. Various expressions crossed her face, and she looked as if she was fighting several conflicting emotions. Finally she stood upright, and moved away from the body. She returned to the table, and placed the knife reverently in the exact centre of the table. Picking up the yellow chalk, she drew another circle around the knife, and then put the chalk down on the edge of the table.

Breathing heavily, but without another glance at Maria she walked around the circle to the steps and climbed up them. At the top Sheila reached without looking for the pull cord and extinguished the cellar light. Using her foot, she pushed the mop bucket to one side and allowed the cellar door to close behind her, leaving the cellar in darkness. Not in total darkness though, for the yellow chalk circles around the kitchen knife and the lifeless body of Maria the cleaner began to glow faintly, casting a thin light on the objects that they surrounded. In the kitchen, Sheila pushed the cellar door fully closed, waiting until she heard the catch click. Then she leant back against the door, and closed her eyes completely. Conflicting expressions ran across her face, and for a moment it seemed that she might cry. Her hands clenched and unclenched.

Another deep breath, and her expression cleared. She walked over to her kettle, picked it up and filled it from the tap at the sink. She looked out across the garden with a considered, enquiring expression, then replaced the kettle and turned it on. She picked up her overnight bag from the table, and walked out of the kitchen. Behind her, the tap continued to run, the water rushing away down the waste pipe of the sink.

Upstairs, Sheila paused on the landing. She looked at the two bedroom doors. With a shudder, she decided that the time had not yet come for her to enter her mother's bedroom, and she opened her own bedroom door instead. She stepped inside, and stopped in shock. The party wall to the house next door - Mister Jones' house - was scratched and torn as if by a thousand claws. The wallpaper was hanging in shreds and chunks of paper and plaster lay on the floor below the hole in the wall that had been opened between the two houses. Her bed however was clear of any debris, and she dropped her overnight bag down beside it. Then she backed out of the room, and closed the door with a trembling hand.

Still backing away, Sheila came to the top of the stairs. She turned and hurried down them. At the bottom of the stairs she glanced towards the front door. The statuette of the unicorn was facing her, and under the weight of her gaze it seemed to tremble slightly. The front door was still coated with grey fingerprint powder, and Sheila frowned. Maria's cleaning materials were still in the kitchen, so she collected them and a cloth. She started to rub away at the fingerprint powder, cursing softly under her breath.

Specks of grey powder fell from the door as she polished. Most fell to the floor but a few drifted past Sheila and landed upon the unicorn. At once, as if stung, Sheila jerked upright. She turned from the door and carefully polished the unicorn, using a corner of her blouse rather than the now marked cloth she had used on the front door. For a long time she stood still; her whole attention fixed on the statuette, one hand gently placed on the back of the statuette. Then she turned away. The silence in the house was immense, and her feet made no impression upon it as she walked slowly back to the kitchen. Sheila opened the door to the cellar, and without looking found the pull cord for the light switch. Her expression fixed, she walked down the stone step and over to the shelving racks. A small selection of candles was on one shelf, and a dusty box of matches.

Sheila picked up six candles, holding them with difficulty. Then she turned and looked at the corpse on the floor, still without emotion in her expression. She placed the first candle on the yellow chalk circle, at the crown of Maria's head. Pacing around the circle, she placed the next opposite the first, below the feet, still on the chalked circle. The other candles she placed equidistant between these first two. Next she walked back to the shelving and picked up the matches. The dust fell from the box, and she casually wiped the back of her hand on her jeans. Kneeling beside the first candle she had placed, Sheila took a match and lit the candle. Using a fresh match for each candle, she repeated the ritual and then replaced the box of matches on the shelf. Without looking back she walked steadily up the stairs, and turned off the electric light before stepping into the kitchen and closing the door.

*

The cellar was left in darkness, apart from the light of the six candles. In the still air the wicks should have burnt with a steady flame, yet the light from the candles moved and the flames danced. Shadows flickered and shifted, met and parted across the roughly cemented walls, finally drawing together in one corner above the discarded skirt. From a central point the shadows took form, became more distinct, a definite shape appeared. A frozen moment in the cold cellar and a shadowman stood against the wall, a horn growing from his forehead. Two faint red points of light appeared, widening in the featureless face, as if twin eyes had opened. Their gaze fell upon Maria's body and the shadowman pulled free from the wall, and stood at the edge of the circle, drinking in the detail before him. The horn bowed forward, the figure moved, and the shadow lay across Maria's corpse.

*

In the kitchen, Sheila leant back against the closed door. Then she walked back into the hall and went towards the front door. Half way along the hall she saw Maria's discarded rosary lying against the wall. She bent to pick it up, but then paused before touching it. She retraced her steps into the kitchen, and returned with the mop in her hands. Reversing the mop, she used the handle to pick up the rosary, holding it carefully at arms' length. She found it hard not to let the beads slip down the handle towards her fingers, and as she made her way back to the kitchen she twice dropped the charm. Each time she picked it up again with the mop's wooden handle, and finally managed to drop the beads into the kitchen waste bin.

She leant the mop against the worktop and then closed the lid of the bin with an expression of relief. Suddenly she realised that the tap was still running, and shaking her head at herself, she turned it off. The telephone in the kitchen rang, and she started in surprise. After it had rung several times, she reluctantly picked up the receiver.

"Is that Miss Balsam?" asked the caller.

"Yes," replied Sheila.

"This is the Cleaning Agency. I just wanted to check that Maria had cleaned everything to your satisfaction as this was, well, a somewhat special job."

"Everything is fine, thank you," said Sheila.

"We would normally have heard back from Maria by now. She isn't still with you, is she?"

"No, she has gone."

"Only she is supposed to check in on completion of special jobs like yours, and she didn't report back to us."

"When I last saw her, she looked like she was about to have a very long sleep."

"Yes, I suppose she would Miss Balsam. May I again express my condolences for your loss?"

"What? Oh, er, yes. Yes, thank you." Sheila replaced the receiver. Walking to the window in the hall, she peered out. There in the street was Maria's car. "I should get rid of that," she said aloud. "But not until after darkness falls." She turned to look at the unicorn statuette, which now again faced the front door. "Or perhaps that should be after darkness rises."

*

"So," Inspector Peake said to the SOCO officer who was standing before his desk, "what you are telling me is that there is no sign of a forced entry to the property, and the fingerprint analysis is worthless to me?" He dropped the thick manila file holding the report onto his desk, where it fell with a thud.

"Well sir," replied Jane, "we aren't saying that. What we are saying is that we can't find any fingerprints that you would not expect. That's slightly different, isn't it?"

Sergeant Wilson had been staring at the desk whilst his superior interrogated the SOCO representative. Now he looked up. "An inside job? A relative?"

"What we can tell you, sir, is that we have found a lot of fingerprints: but from a very small number of people. We have identified the victim's of course. And her daughter. But there is nothing that we can give you at the moment that is going to point you in other directions. Maybe the autopsy report will help you more?"

"That," said Inspector Peake morosely, "is only going to tell me that she was impaled by something that went right through her and was then taken away. And you didn't find it in the house."

"If we didn't find it, sir, it is because it wasn't there."

"Unlike the victim. Who was there, so at least you found her."

Sergeant Wilson intervened. "Jane, did you search the grounds?"

"Grounds?" asked Peake. "There's a garden. One front, one back. And a house next door owned by a crafty beggar that I don't like, who has been mixed up in too many unresolved cases on my list already. Did you search his garden, too?"

"We didn't have a warrant," replied Jane. "But we did check both gardens. No sign of anything being disturbed recently - buried, that is - and nothing anyone could have used as a weapon like that. There was a recently deceased cat, but we don't think that is significant."

"Wilson, you've seen the daughter," Inspector Peake said. "Do you think she's capable of running her mother through with… what do we think it is? A spear, for godssake?"

Wilson thought carefully. "She's got it in her, I'd say, boss. But is she strong enough? That's another matter."

"I do some martial arts training," offered Jane.

Inspector Peake looked uninterested. "So what?"

"There's small bloke there who could run a spear through anything. Or anybody."

"One of those Kung Fu types, is he?" asked Wilson.

"No, he works in the supermarket. Says it is all about focus and desire and intent, not about strength."

"So if her daughter wanted to kill her mother enough, she could do it? Like that?" asked Wilson.

Peake became very interested. "First on the scene too. Always makes her a suspect in my book. Killing her mother: could be one of those Greek myth things?"

"Or maybe her mother was just a nasty piece of work," suggested Wilson. "Some of these statements I've read from the neighbours point that way. Yes, it's all this 'don't speak ill of the dead' rubbish in there, but there are some hints that she treated her daughter like some sort of slave."

"A weapon," said Inspector Peake. "We need a weapon. You didn't search Mister Jones' garden, you said?"

"Not the back garden, no. A quick look, that's all. We did look over the front garden too, but that's all open and there was nothing there and nowhere to hide anything."

"Well go and look now, then."

"What about a warrant, sir?"

"Jones will let you look round his garden. He won't want me hauling him back in here for half a day, so he'll let you in: unless he's involved in some way. In which case I shall be delighted to spend some time asking him questions. Tell you what, take one of the murder team lads with you. Might smooth your path a bit. That Ian Evans knows Jones, take him."

"Where will I find him, sir?"

"In the canteen," replied Wilson. "Best place to find anyone in this place. Especially at lunch time. It's warm and there's lots of tea. He'll say 'no' to you, though."

"What?" Jane looked confused.

"Going to Mister Jones' place who wouldn't?" agreed Peake. "But Evans can do it. If he says 'No' to you twice, tell him he's to come straight to my office with his notebooks. And they had better be up to date…"

Wilson laughed.

"Off you go!" ordered Peake.

Jane nodded, and walked out of the office with some relief. It was no fun being the most junior member of the SOCO team: jobs like this always seemed to fall on her shoulders. She walked along the corridor from Inspector Peake's office, and descended the stairs. The canteen was on the ground floor, and was half full of various police officers. Jane stopped by the table nearest to the door, which was occupied by two detectives arguing over a report form.

"'Scuse me. Either of you two know an Ian Evans?"

"On his own over there." One of the detectives pointed at a solitary uniformed constable who was drinking coffee and reading a newspaper at a table against the wall.

Jane approached the table and pulled out a chair. "Can I join you?" she asked.

The constable looked up, and Jane saw his eyes check out the identity tag on the cord around her neck. "Do I know you?" asked Evans.

"No, but Inspector Peake told me to come and ask you to accompany me on a site visit."

"Really?" Evans dropped his newspaper. "Nothing Peake asks me to do ever turns out well. Where am I supposed to take you?"

Jane reached into her pocket and pulled out a sheet of paper. She unfolded it, and pushed it across the table. Ian Evans turned it round, and took one look. He pushed it back across the table to Jane.

"No," he said. Evans picked up his newspaper, and vanished behind it. "No," he said again from the depths of the paper.

Jane swallowed. "Peake said that if you told me 'No' twice, you had to immediately go to his office with all your notebooks for inspection."

Evans slammed the newspaper down on the canteen table. "He means it then? What do you want with Mister Jones?"

"Well, you know that a woman was killed at the house next door to him?"

"Yes. I've been making sure that I've been busy doing stuff that kept me well away."

Jane gave Evans an odd look, but carried on. "Well Peake wants me to go and check Mister Jones' back garden again to see if a weapon could have been concealed there."

"Why you?" asked Evans. "Why not send a couple of uniformed bodies down to scout around, if the main search team didn't look somewhere?"

"He is: that's you. I got roped in because he didn't like the report my boss gave him."

Evans laughed then, briefly and without mirth. "Sounds like Peake. All right, there's no getting out of it I suppose." He stood and beckoned Jane to follow him. "We'll go and see if there's a spare car from the pool to use."

Jane followed Evans out of the canteen and down the hall to the main desk. The desk sergeant consulted a wall board and shook his head. "You're out of luck, Evans. Everything is in use at the moment, mainly out on your boss' stuff."

Evans scowled. "We'll have to use mine then," he said to Jane and led the way out of the police station into the staff car park.

"Sorry about the mess," he said insincerely as he unlocked the car. "Just chuck the papers onto the back seat."

Jane did as she was told and cleared enough room to make the front seat usable. She watched as Evans pulled out his notebook, and jotted down the mileage reading.

"Peake's a demon for checking expenses claims," Evans explained. "He likes to keep us all on top of this stuff. What's your boss like?"

"No easier, really," replied Jane. "So, what's this Mister Jones like then? No one seems to have anything good to say about him. Has he got history or form?"

"Ha! History! Oh yes, he's got history. But form? No. Never been accused of anything. But if there is anything really strange going on round here he seems to be mixed up in it somewhere. And nothing he gets near ever gets officially cleared up. That's why Peake hates him. There's all these cases floating about on Peake's record which will never be officially closed, and it doesn't make Peake look good."

"You keep saying never officially closed?"

"Yes. Officially. Unofficially, everyone knows that they are never going anywhere and no other Inspector will agree to put a finger on the files. The Higher Ups won't order them to because it is easier to just bury the files on Peake's clear up record and say nothing. Nobody is ever going to unearth them or complain. Well, except Peake, of course."

"Oh."

"That's why you won't find anyone keen to get involved with Jones. Or to have anything to do with him. That's why Peake told you to blackmail me, or I'd never have taken you out to the house. I've been on a few of those cases, and that's why my promotion never seems to turn up."

Evans stopped the car at the exit to the car park, looked both ways and turned out into the traffic. "What's the brief again?"

"We don't have a warrant, but Peake wants the back garden of Jones' house examining in case there's something there that could have been a murder weapon."

"Yes! Peake would love to get a chance to get Mister Jones on something like that. But we all know he's not going to turn out to be the guilty party. Jones isn't like that."

"Can you tell that about someone?" asked Jane.

"I've met Jones a few times," replied Evans, negotiating a busy junction. "He's no killer. He's a lot of things, but not that. Look, there's the house now."

Evans turned into the side road he was looking for. About half way down, a solitary police car was parked outside a house. "I know that your team has finished," said Evans. "That poor bloke was sent here this morning just to keep any reporters off the doorstep. And souvenir hunters, of course."

Jane nodded. Evans drew to a halt behind the marked police car, and got out of his vehicle. He knocked on the window of the marked car, and muttered briefly to the driver, who returned to his examination of the football news in his newspaper.

"Come on!" called Evans, and Jane scrambled out of the car. "I'll do the talking," Evans told her.

"But Peake told me... started Jane.

"Peake knew I'd sort this. That's why he told you to get me."

Evans unlatched the metal gate, and walked down the path to Mister Jones' front door. He looked back, and once satisfied that Jane was following him, he banged hard on the door. It was opened very quickly.

"Why, Ian! This is a nice surprise!" said Mister Jones.

"Mister Jones, this is my colleague, Jane.... Jane. It's about the unfortunate event next door."

"Ah, yes. Mrs Balsam. Her daughter has been stopping with me whilst, well, you know. Is it her you want to see?"

"No, actually it's your back garden. The search team report is a bit cursory there, and Inspector Peake wants us to have another look. Do you mind?"

"Of course not, Ian. It is my civic duty, and as you know, I'm always ready to help the police."

Jane stared at Mister Jones when he said that, but could not detect any hint of sarcasm in the tone.

"Come on Jane," said Evans, and started to walk around the side of the house.

"Do I come too?" asked Mister Jones.

"Better not, just in case we do find anything. I'm not expecting to of course," replied Evans over his shoulder, "but something could have been thrown over the fence."

"And if that's the case sir," said Jane, "we need to preserve the evidence trail."

"Oh, I see," replied Mister Jones. "I'll leave you to get on with it, then."

Evans led Jane to the back of the house, and they looked around the garden. The signs of the storm were everywhere in the blown leaves, scattered twigs, and of course in the missing fence panel.

"I wonder where that is?" asked Jane, looking at the gap in the fence.

Evans pointed to the broken piece of panelling that had been dragged over to the garden shed. "Kicked down, or blown down?" he asked aloud.

Jane shrugged. "No way to know until I examine it, if it's worth that."

"What do you want to do first?" asked Evans.

"Down the side of the fence, checking in the bushes that grow alongside the fence. Then across the bottom of the garden, back up this side, and then a quick look in the shed."

"Surely this was done the first day, though?" asked Evans.

"Yes, but for some reason it wasn't properly documented, so that's why we're here again."

"Well you take that side, I'll take this, and we'll meet in the middle."

Jane walked over to the gap in the fence between the two gardens, and peered through at the house next door. The windows were blank, but then he thought that he saw a face at the kitchen window.

"I say! There's someone in there!" she called to Evans.

"Probably the owner or the cleaner, then," replied Evans, uninterested.

Jane stared at the window, but the face had gone.

"Didn't look like a woman's face. It was much harder than that. But it was shadowed, so I didn't see it clearly."

Evan ignored her, and walked slowly down the side of the garden. Despite his uninterested attitude, he still examined the ground very carefully. He shuddered slightly at the sight of a recently killed cat, which seemed to have been torn apart. At last he arrived at the bottom of the garden, and turned to go across the line of flowerbeds beside the fence that marked the bottom of the garden. "Did anyone do the gardens on the other side?" he called.

Jane was still walking slowly down the line of the missing fence panel that separated the two adjoining houses. There were several shrubs and bushes planted there, and he methodically moved the branches of each to check the soil below them for any sign of disturbance. "Don't know. But it's not on my job list for today." He saw a line of footprints crossing the soil bed, and heading for the house next door. He looked up, and there was a face at the window in the kitchen door.

Evans took hold of the top of the fence with both hands, and tested it gingerly. Once convinced that it would take his weight, he pulled himself up until he could peer over the top of the fence. He could see nothing of interest, and dropped back down again. He looked round, and Jane was gone.

"Oi! Where are you?" he called, but apart from a brief echo, the garden was silent and empty.

Chapter Seven

The kitchen seemed empty when Jane peered through the door. The outside of the window was dirty, and in consequence her view was obscured. However, she still put out her hand to the door handle. Almost before she had touched it, the latch made a loud click, and the door swung open a little. Jane stepped back in surprise, then reached out and slowly pushed the door. It swung open properly.

"Hello?" called Jane.

The house was silent.

"Hello?" she called again. Her voice did not seem to echo normally, as you would expect in an empty house, but in some way seemed to be muffled.

Jane suddenly felt a great reluctance to walk through the door whilst at the same time a compulsion to do so impelled her to take a step forward.

"Miss Balsam?" she called. Her words fell softly, as stones on a mossy bank.

Jane stepped inside the kitchen, and looked around. She had been busy herself inside the house the day before, yet all seemed strange and somehow different. She looked around, but without a body on the floor the kitchen had a different atmosphere: although still not a nice atmosphere. She could feel a sense of heaviness, of unhappiness and especially of unfinished business hanging in the air so palpably she could almost taste it.

She looked at the floor where the body of the late Mrs Balsam had lain. The tiles had been thoroughly cleaned, and no mark or stain remained. The deep scores and marks in the cupboard door of course remained vivid and disturbing. The doors had light coloured surfaces, and the dark interior wood, stained still where blood had splashed and dried, stood out clearly. She walked over to the damaged door, and tentatively put out her hand. Her fingers touched the deep grooves and explored their depth and feel.

The wood felt rough beneath her fingertips, and she jumped as a splinter jabbed into one finger. She jerked her hand away, the splinter tearing roughly at her flesh. Jane sucked the finger until the blood stopped flowing, and glared at the door. Some of her own blood gleamed there, fresh against the dark interior wood and limed-oak surface of the cupboard door. She jammed a hand into her pocket, and pulled out a tissue: she wiped the absorbent paper on the door, cleaning away the bright trail of her blood that trickled down the limed-oak front of the cupboard door. Deep within the scores and indentations some of her blood still gleamed fresh and bright red, but she ignored it.

Close to a tall storage cupboard was the kitchen bin. Jane stepped over to the bin, and after opening it she dropped the bloodied tissue into the bin. After closing the lid she realised that there had been no disposable bag lining the bin, but immediately forgot about that.

The windows had been cleaned of fingerprint powder, and

when she glanced through she could see across the garden into the garden next door. Faintly she could make out the shape of Ian Evans as the constable walked slowly along the line of the far fence. Somehow it was reassuring to see the familiar uniform, not so very far away. She scowled at his faint reflection before turning away.

Jane went back to the damaged cupboard door, and this time knelt down close to the marks. She peered at them closely without touching them. "Whatever could have made these?" she said aloud.

In the corner of the kitchen closest to the door into the hall, some shadows started to gather and collect.

She peered at the marks from several different angles, then whistled softly. "This took some force," she said aloud. "What ever was used here was driven first through the body, then into this wood. Whatever could have done that? Whoever could have done that?"

The light in the kitchen faded a little, and the pool of shadows darkened, and then slowly began to grow up the wall. At the top of the shadows a sharp point appeared, and elongated.

Jane fell into a reverie, focussed entirely upon the cupboard door, and oblivious to the threat growing at her back. The dimming of the light went unnoticed. The shadow shape became defined now as the hard, strong body of a man: but a man with a horn growing from his forehead. As Jane gazed at the door two eyes opened, and features not previously seen became clear: a nose, eyebrows, and a cruel mouth without a hint of warmth or pity.

The shadowman moved slightly on the wall, focussing upon the figure kneeling before it. The horn began to dip, and the atmosphere in the kitchen became intense.

The loud ringtone of the mobile telephone in Jane's jacket pocket broke the gathering spell. Jane stood up and as she did so the definition of the shadowman wavered and became less distinct before drawing back in upon itself. The horn faded.

Jane pulled the phone from her pocket and pressed the green 'answer' button.

"Where in hell are you!" demanded Ian Evans, his voice thin and buzzing through the small speaker.

"What?"

"Jane, where are you? We were searching Jones' garden, and then you were gone!"

"Oh, sorry, Mr Evans. There's nothing to worry about. I'm fine."

"Where are you then?"

"Well, I saw a face at the kitchen window of the house, you know, the Balsam's, so I came to knock on the door and check all was all right."

"You do not just leave a search scene, especially without telling the other officers were you are going. Have you forgotten all your training?"

"Yes, you're right, sorry," apologised Jane.

Evans was a little mollified, but only a little. "So, was every thing all right?"

"Well actually, it is a bit odd. I know that I saw someone here, but the house is empty. Unlocked, and empty."

"Well, if that's the case you shouldn't be inside there. You don't have a warrant card, and even if you did, strictly you would still be trespassing!"

Jane looked all around the kitchen, which seemed brighter than it had. She blinked, and decided that a shadow or a cloud must have passed over the sun. "Well, if it is empty, it is unsecured. Should I just make sure that there are no burglars or press in here?"

"You can stay just where you are!" ordered Evans. "If you go poking about, then you are going to get into serious trouble there, and you are so not going to drag me into that."

"I won't get you in bother, Mr Evans."

"Well stay just where you are. I'm going to come over there myself: at least that will give you a bit of respectability." Evans hung up, and Jane dropped her phone back into her pocket.

The kitchen was no longer of such interest to her, and she glanced casually around, before looking at the open door to the hall. "Really, it can't do any harm, can it?" she asked herself. "Never mind what Evans says. It can't hurt if I just look into the hall at least. I mean, what if there had been a break-in and I didn't check? What would my boss say to me then?"

Jane looked out of the kitchen window towards the gap in the fence. Through the streaks on the window left by the storm she could see the figure of Constable Evans striding purposefully towards her, although he had not yet left Mister Jones' garden or crossed the flower beds that lay across the line of the missing fence panel. Her attention was drawn then by a small sound from the hall.

A shiver ran down her back. Maybe she was not alone in the house after all. Yet she had shouted aloud when she originally walked through the kitchen door: so maybe whoever had made that noise was not here legitimately. That alone would both excuse and justify her coming into the house. Evans was only moments away if she needed help, so she set her shoulders and stepped boldly out into the hall. The stairs were empty and still, so she looked down the length of the hall towards the front door. The unicorn statuette faced down the length of the hall. It was now a deeper shade of terracotta than she recalled, and the horn seemed more menacing. Somehow more menacing yet was the still figure of Sheila Balsam. She stood with one hand on the statuette, facing her with an icy expression that froze Jane to the spot.

"Exactly who are you, and what are you doing in my home?" she demanded haughtily.

"Oh, oh, please excuse me," stammered Jane.

"Who are you? And by what right have you invaded here?" Sheila asked again.

She still had not moved, other than to speak, and Jane suddenly began to feel very uneasy about this woman. She had previously seen her as a relative, devastated by her loss and as a less than forceful person. The change was abrupt and disconcerting.

She was very relieved when she heard the back door open, and the heavy boots worn by Ian Evans sounded on the kitchen tiles. Evans' entry into the hall as a uniformed policeman seemed to lower the tension a little.

"Ah, Miss Balsam," said Evans on seeing her standing by the front door. "I must apologise for our intrusion."

"What is going on?" asked Sheila, but in a more moderate tone.

"We are both police officers," replied Evans, stretching the point slightly to cover Jane's legal position. "We were conducting a search in the garden next door when Jane here thought she saw an intruder."

"Yes," added Jane gratefully. "So I checked the back door, and called out several times. When there was no reply, I thought I had better just make sure that the property was secure before leaving, well, with what happened."

"Oh, I see," replied Sheila. She visibly relaxed. "Thank you for your consideration. I must not have heard you call out. But as you can see, I'm fine and all is well."

"Yes, glad to see it," Evans said quickly. "So now we will get out of your way."

"Are you sure that I cannot press you stay?" asked Sheila. She still had not moved, nor taken her left hand from the unicorn statuette. "Tea, perhaps? Or coffee?"

"Thank you, no," said Evans firmly. He reached out and took Jane by the arm. Jane seemed fascinated by the tableau before her, and unwilling to move, but Evans tugged firmly at her arm. "We should leave. Now." He practically hissed the last word into

Jane's ear, and the SOCO officer seemed to surface from a dream.

"What? Oh, yes, of course. Miss, I'm sorry if I disturbed you or worried you at all."

"Oh, I wasn't concerned about me," replied Sheila. She took one hand from the unicorn, and walked slowly down the hall towards them. Evans tugged Jane urgently and the two stepped backwards into the kitchen. Evans glanced over his shoulder, and checked that the back door was still open. He pulled Jane across the kitchen floor and out through the back door, closing it as they left.

"What did you do that for?" demanded Jane as soon as their feet were on the grass.

"There was something in there that wasn't right," said Evans tersely. He continued to walk backwards across the garden until he reached the flower beds. Those he jumped over, landing heavily on the grass in Mister Jones' garden. "Now get here with me if you don't want to get into deeper water than you'd like!" he ordered.

Jane followed him into the other garden, although she walked across the flowerbeds, carelessly trampling on a number of bedding plants as she went. "Why did you pull me out of there like that?" she demanded, suddenly angry.

"Because there was something in there I didn't like," replied Evans shortly. "And a policeman has to learn to follow his instincts. Now, you've got that fenceline to search yet. Get on with it."

"What are you going to do, then?"

"Me?" asked Evans. "I'm going to work out what to say to Inspector Peake to save your backside if she rings up and makes a complaint. And I'm going to have a quick check in Jones' garden shed so that I can tell Peake we looked everywhere when we go back to the station and report."

With that Evans turned on his heel and walked across to the door of the elderly garden shed. Jane watched him go. She shook her head, knowing that Evans was right. Jane looked across again at the kitchen of the house next door. Once again she could see the flash of a dark face against the glass of the window, but this time she felt no compulsion to go and investigate. Instead Jane turned her attention to the fence, and walked slowly and purposefully down towards the end of Mister Jones' garden. Her eyes were fixed on the ground, but her thoughts were elsewhere.

*

The knock on my front door had distracted me from the task I had been about to undertake. However it needed doing and so after closing the front door I walked back up the stairs to the front bedroom. The dustpan, brush and rubbish bag lay on the floor where I had dropped them when I had been disturbed. I walked around the guest bed, now stripped of the bedding that I had already placed in the washing machine.

Feeling unusually domestic, I bent to the task of sweeping flakes and larger pieces of broken plaster from the floor. Only as I started to empty the bits into the bin bag did I realise that as well as plaster and pieces of plasterboard, there were fragments of brick and cement or mortar mixed with the debris on the floor. Glad of the chance to ease my back, I straightened up and surveyed the wall. The plaster was cracked across, but except for the hole in the wall itself and the fallen plaster around it, there was in fact little damage.

As I was about to bend back down to my task, a flicker of movement on the other side of the hole distracted me. With unwitting curiosity and careless of the effect of the debris on my trousers, I knelt down and put an eye to the wall. A blue eye on the other side regarded me, and with a cry of alarm I fell back against the bed. I could hear soft laughter from the room in the house next door.

"Why, Mister Jones, did I startle you?" came Sheila's voice from the other bedroom.

"Sheila? Yes, a bit, I must admit."

"Well then, it is your own fault for peering into a girl's bedroom, Mister Jones."

"I was just cleaning up in here," I told her.

"Of course you were."

"Is there much damage on your side, Sheila?" I asked.

"Not really anything to worry about."

"Good," I replied. "I wonder what caused this?"

"Storm damage I expect," Sheila said in an offhand tone.

I surveyed the hole. Storm damage seemed to me to be the

most unlikely cause of this very specific destruction.

"It's only a little hole," Sheila continued. "I'm sure that it won't take much to fix it."

"I thought I might have to knock some more plaster off the wall and then replace the whole piece of plasterboard," I admitted.

"Mister Jones!" There was an odd note in Sheila's voice I neither recognised nor understood at that moment. "A girl cannot sleep in her bedroom with a hole like that in the wall. Why, who knows what might happen!"

"Sheila!" I was shocked. This was not the quiet mousy girl next door I had been accustomed to speak to upon occasion, but then I reflected that her mother's passing might have released or dissipated some long held insecurities in her personality. It seemed a little soon for that sort of change to occur, though. "You know that this is my guest room! I don't sleep here!"

"But I sleep on this side, Mister Jones. As I think you know, don't you?"

I really did not know how to reply to that. There was a moment of silence whilst I thought about it. "Sheila, I'm going to have the hole covered here on this side. But would it make you feel more comfortable if I come round and do something about the hole from your side?"

Suddenly her voice was more akin to the Sheila I recognised. It was hesitant, unsure and self-conscious. "Oh no, Mister Jones. No, I wouldn't want that. I mean, this is my room. It's my place, my secure place. No one comes in here!"

"I'm sorry. I don't want to intrude."

Her bright, coquettish tone resumed at once. "Oh, I'm so sure that you don't want to do that..." She was silent for a few moments, and through the hole between our homes I could hear her breathing. Then her voice changed back again. "Mister Jones, have you seen Molly our cat? I haven't seen her since, well, you know."

"No Sheila, I'm sorry. I haven't seen your cat. I'll keep an eye out for her though, and if I do see her I'll try and tempt her in here and then you can come round for her."

"Thank you, Mister Jones. You really are quite a nice person, aren't you?"

I was taken aback. "Thank you, Sheila. I do try, but I don't think that it's true at all."

There was a laugh again from the other bedroom, a laugh that suddenly seemed to take on a mocking tone. "I will spare your blushes, Mister Jones. I'll sleep in the big bedroom at the back of the house tonight. Actually, I will probably move in there anyway now that I have the house to myself at last."

I wondered why Sheila seemed to be avoiding the use of her mother's name, but thought that grief worked in strange ways and it might be best not to mention the matter. After all, it was not strictly my business.

Again, she gave that slightly mocking laugh. "So if you did have any notions about peering through the peepy hole tonight, you will be disappointed, won't you?"

"Sheila! I assure you! I would just never think of doing that!"

"No, no you probably wouldn't. Shame."

"I don't understand…"

"I know. Why don't you come round a bit later? Keep me company."

I was silent. I was very uncomfortable with this girl, well this woman, who should be grieving but instead seemed to slip between two very different personalities.

"I'm not sure."

"Mister Jones, that's very ungallant of you, not to want to show support for a lady in some distress. Besides there's someone else here who is quite keen to meet you."

"I thought you were on your own, and that's why you wanted company?" I asked, now completely confused.

"Well, I am now." Her tone was suddenly brisk and business-like. "But Maria, the cleaner, she's on her own and I thought that she really liked the look of you. You should really come round a bit later and meet her."

"Your cleaner?"

"I never thought of you as a snob!"

"It's not that, Sheila. Just that I don't think I've ever met her."

"I think that she's probably hungry for some company right now, Mister Jones. You'd do very well for her."

"Errrrr," was all I could manage to say.

"So that's settled."

There was a brief movement of air through the hole in the wall. Either brisk movement had caused a draught, or Sheila had blown a kiss through the hole. I ventured to put my eye back to the hole in the wall, but as far as I could see, the room was empty. But it did not feel empty, and as I returned to my task of sweeping up, I had the uncomfortable itch between the shoulder blades that means our ancient survival instincts are warning us that we are being observed, or possibly stalked, by a predator. I was unaccountably relieved when at last the task was finished. With some difficulty, I picked up the heavy rubbish bag and walked out of the front bedroom. The feeling of being watched did not leave me until I closed the bedroom door behind me.

I put down the bag. At the end of the landing was a small window that looked out across the front garden. I walked along the landing, and leaning on the small windowledge with both hands, I peered out along the street. I could see the marked police patrol car outside Sheila's house, and the car I recognised as Ian Evan's own car parked outside mine. Behind the patrol car was an older vehicle. It had been there now for some time I recalled, and had to assume that it belonged to Maria, the cleaner who was apparently so keen to see me.

*

Inspector Peake stared hard at Constable Evans and Jane, the SOCO officer. "So, you found nothing?" he asked.

"Nothing, sir," agreed Evans. "We checked the fence line thoroughly, and Jones' garden shed too. Nothing."

"Right," said Peake decisively. He opened the file again, and flicked through some statements without really reading them. "This is what we have: The late Mrs Balsam. Dead. Very unlikely to be a self inflicted wound, wouldn't you agree, Wilson?"

Sergeant Wilson nodded. "The chances of Mrs Balsam committing suicide like that are slim."

"So, she has been killed, unlawfully, by person or persons unknown," continued Inspector Peake. "The weapon has been removed. There is no sign of a forced entry. Your boss is sure of that, miss?"

Jane agreed. "No damage on any doors, sir. And as you can see, the number of fingerprints on the doors and windows are very limited."

"So who has just become suspect number one?" Peake asked softly.

"The daughter," agreed Sergeant Wilson.

"The daughter," Peake confirmed. "Evans, go get her, please. She's not being charged because we don't have any evidence yet. There's no need to frighten her or anything, let's just ask to go over her statement. Check her fingerprints, that sort of thing."

Wilson stood up. Peake looked up at him. "Wilson, sit down. I want her here nice and quiet and unconcerned. Evans, you go and get her. No arrest for questioning, just ask her politely to come here to make another statement."

"What if she refuses, sir?" asked Ian Evans.

"Then you walk quietly back to your car and you ring me. I'll decide then what I'm going to do."

"Perhaps she would come in more easily if I go with Constable Evans?" asked Jane suddenly.

The three police officers looked at her with surprise.

"You are a SOCO officer," Peake pointed out. "You don't have power of arrest."

"But that's not what you want, is it? And she's seen me before."

"Actually, it's not a bad idea, is it?" mused Wilson. "We don't want her thinking she's a suspect, do we? Jane here could explain how some fingerprints were smudged, and we need to retake Miss Balsam's prints to help us rule out her involvement."

Peake smiled. "That I like! Right, off you go, then." He went back to his file, this time with more interest. After a moment he looked up. "You two still here?" he asked more sharply.

"Just going, sir," replied Evans.

He and Jane left the office. When the door was closed, and they were safely someway down the corridor and hopefully out of earshot, he stopped and turned to the SOCO officer.

"What do you think you are playing at?" he demanded.

"I don't know what you mean, Constable Evans. Or may I call

you Ian?"

"I want to know what you were thinking of, suggesting that you come with me on this call."

"I just wanted to make a positive contribution, Ian."

Evans made an exasperated noise. "Like you did when we went to Jones' house? And you ended up at the crime scene?"

"Well that turned out all right, didn't it?"

Evans looked at her in astonishment. "How can you say that? You illegally entered a house, and worse, got caught!"

Jane shrugged. "And we are both still here, aren't we?"

"It's amazing we are both still in a job!"

Jane started walking down the corridor away from Evans.

"Where do you think you are going now?" demanded Evans, hurrying to catch her up.

Jane smiled at him demurely. "Why, to your car, Constable Evans. We have a direct instruction from Inspector Peake. I'm sure that you do not want to disobey him, do you?"

Evans caught her roughly by the arm and stopped her walking. She threw his hand off her arm with an angry gesture.

"Don't touch me!" she spat at him.

Taken aback by the sudden change, Ian Evans peered intently at her face, and she stepped backwards, averting her eyes.

"I want to know why you are so interested in going back to the Balsam house," insisted Evans.

"Why, in order to obey the orders of a superior, Constable Evans. I suggest you follow my example," Jane replied harshly. Then her demure expression returned, and she smiled sweetly at him. "Don't you want to spend time in your car with a pretty girl, then?"

She walked away again, and this time Evans followed her down to the car park. This time however, he had an uneasy expression and some troubled thoughts. In the past two years Evans had twice found himself involved in work, and with people, that were other than ordinary: this affair he felt had the same taint and he was becoming very uneasy. Evans unlocked his car, and Jane climbed into the front passenger seat. She wrinkled her nose in disgust.

"Were you really planning to get Miss Balsam to climb in here, Ian Evans?" she asked. Jane got back out of the car as Evans got into the driving seat. She leant forward to look at him, and despite his reservations about the SOCO officer, Evans found himself enjoying the view.

"Wait!" she commanded, and walked back into the police station.

Evans sighed. He seemed to have little choice. However, only a short time passed before Jane returned, carrying a large black bin bag.

"What's that for?" Evans asked.

"And I thought you were a detective!" replied Jane. She promptly picked up the worst of the rubbish from the inside of the car, newspapers, magazines, fast food cartons and discarded sweet wrappers, and threw them into the rubbish bag. She tied the top securely, and walked around to the rear of the car. Jane opened the boot, wrinkled her nose in distaste and dropped the bag into the boot. Closing the lid with a bang that made Evans wince, she returned to the front seat, closing the door behind her.

"What are you waiting for?" she asked. "Don't want to be late, do we?"

Despite himself, Evans had to laugh. He started the engine, and reversed carefully out of the parking bay. The drive to the Balsam's house seemed to be a shorter journey every time he took the trip, he reflected: even though this journey was conducted in complete silence. Jane looked out of the side window, and was reluctant to look at Evans, and after his first halting attempts to start a conversation were rebuffed with silence, he stopped trying. When the car stopped, however, Jane returned to a livelier mood.

"Whose car is that?" she asked, pointing to an elderly hatchback parked behind the marked patrol car, whose occupant was still on duty to deter the single remaining member of the press who waited in the hope of an interesting photo opportunity.

Evans shrugged. "The cleaner's I think. You lot sometimes leave a bit of a mess behind you, don't you?"

Jane laughed. "I suppose we do. I've never thought about it, really." She opened her door and climbed out of the car.

Evans followed her example. He tugged down his uniform

jacket, and settled his cap more comfortably on his head.

"Should you wear that at a more jaunty angle?" asked Jane.

Evans gave her a blank, professional look. "No," he replied, shortly. "Come on." He walked to the gate at the end of the drive, and opened it. The uniformed officer in the marked patrol car gave him a hard look, then waved. Evans waved back as Jane swept past him through the open gate.

"Thank you," she said brightly.

"Me first," insisted Evans as they approached the front door.

"But of course, Constable," replied Jane.

Evans shot her a very stern look, and she giggled slightly.

"Sorry," she apologised. "I seem to be a little nervous."

"Let me do the talking," replied Evans, and knocked hard on the front door. Inside the house, the echoes ran away down the hall. Evans knocked again.

"Let me try," suggested Jane.

Evans looked at her in astonishment. "What difference will that make?" he asked.

Jane smiled at him, and reached for the door knocker. She tapped it twice, not as hard as Evans had done, yet both officers felt that the sound from the door was of a different quality: more insistent and urgent. Evans again gave Jane a very assessing look.

"There's something different about you," he said aloud.

"You are probably just not used to attractive girls, Constable Evans," replied Jane.

Before Ian Evans could reply, the door opened, and Sheila Balsam looked at them.

"Ah, you two again?" she asked. "The police officers from earlier?"

"Er, well, yes," replied Evans. "Miss Balsam, we've been ordered by Inspector Peake to ask you to come down to the police station for a short interview."

Sheila sighed. "Constable, it is very inconvenient. I am waiting for a delivery. An important delivery."

"Miss Balsam, the Inspector was very insistent. It is rather important."

"So is my delivery."

"How can it be more important than the investigation into whoever killed your mother?" Evans asked her.

Sheila looked as if she might start crying, and leaned against the door for support.

"That's enough," said Jane suddenly. "Miss Balsam, Constable Evans here has been insensitive, and I'm terribly sorry. But it is really important."

"Really important?"

"Well, yes," replied Jane. "Look, if you like, you go with Constable Evans here and I'll wait for your delivery. I'll leave the package here in the hall, then lock up and leave, or wait for you if you'd prefer?"

"That's very kind of you," replied Sheila uncertainly. Then she made a decision. "Very well, I'll get my coat. The delivery is of some chairs. The men know where they are to go, so if you let them in and lock up later? Oh, and my cleaner is still somewhere about so if you make sure that she has gone before you leave?"

"Of course I will," replied Jane.

Evans looked at the two women in confusion. "Can the cleaner not let your delivery people in, Miss Balsam? Since she's here?"

"Well," replied Sheila, "She's not terribly good with people, and also she might not want to wait if they are a bit late. I'll just pick up my coat..." Sheila Balsam reached behind the front door and produced a coat and a handbag, seemingly from nowhere. "Right, Constable. Off we go." Sheila walked away from the door down the drive towards the marked police car.

"Well, don't let her get away!" Jane told Evans.

"This just isn't right!" objected Evans.

Jane stepped into the hall, where the afternoon shadows fell across her face and obscured her expression. She stood beside the unicorn, and placed her right hand on it. "The house will still be here when you bring Miss Balsam back, Constable Evans. Off you go now."

Evans didn't see Jane move, but the front door swung firmly shut in his face. Left with no choice, he followed Sheila Balsam up the drive and away from the front door and its mysteries.

*

Sometime later, Andy Parris, the local newspaper's photographer, became alert. He was sitting on a garden wall opposite the Balsam's house, smoking a cigarette and drinking coffee from a Styrofoam cup, whilst listening to an audio book to stay his growing ennui. This assignment had left him feeling bored and listless. The affair had not attracted national interest: that meant he was not rubbing shoulders with the press photographers from the national daily newspapers, or better yet - their colleagues from the TV and radio world.

At first he had been flattered, then mildly insulted by the presence of the marked police car. "At least it hasn't rained," he grumbled to himself, and then half closed his eyes and concentrated on listening to the audio book.

He almost missed the undramatic moment when the front door of the Balsam house opened. Maria walked out of the door and strode down the drive. Her hair was mussed up, and her clothes were a little awry, yet she walked with a steady purpose. She had a pair of reflective sunglasses that looked a little incongruous on her. The day was bright enough to warrant sunglasses but the pair she wore would have been more appropriate on a ski slope than a suburban street. Parris promptly grabbed his camera, and took several pictures. The camera was set for both auto focus and continuous shooting, so he had several pictures of Maria as she approached the garden gate.

Parris turned off his audio book, and jumped down from the garden wall. He plastered an insincere, but winning, smile across his face and walked across the road to accost Maria. As he did so, the uniformed constable swiftly got out of the marked police car.

"Miss!" called the policeman to Maria.

She stopped walking and looked at the policeman, without replying.

"This gentleman is from the press," said the constable.

Maria gave Parris a considering look that made him feel uneasy, but intrigued.

"If you don't want to talk to him, or don't want your photo taken, or just don't want him bothering you, say so and I'll deal with him," continued the constable.

Andy Parris looked at the police officer in surprise, and then realised that the constable was probably every bit as bored as he was, and was welcoming even this short distraction in his otherwise very dull shift.

Maria waved her left hand dismissively at the constable. Looking disappointed, he reluctantly went back to the police car and vanished inside. Briefly the crackle of voices from the police radio could be heard as the car door was opened and closed, then the street was quiet again. Maria looked at Parris.

"Excuse me, but are you connected with the house here?" asked Parris, pushing his camera to one side, and frowning briefly as the strap holding the camera around his neck snagged on his collar.

Maria did not reply, but nodded.

"Would you mind if I asked you a few questions?" asked Parris.

Maria shook her head and turned away towards what Parris realised must be her own car.

"I'm sure that my editor would happily pay you some money for your time."

Maria reached the bonnet of her car without looking back at him as he walked after her along the pavement.

"Doesn't have to be here," Parris added. "I could come with you to a place of your choosing, and there we could talk about the house and what went on?"

Maria stopped beside the small hatchback, clearly considering the suggestion.

"My car is just here," Parris said in an encouraging tone. You drive wherever you like, and I'll follow you, then we can talk?"

Maria stepped along the side of her car and opened the passenger door, in a clear invitation. Still she had not spoken, and Parris felt uneasy again. He shivered, as if a cloud had passed across the sun.

"Someone walked across my grave, as my grandmother used to say," he muttered. "Still, in for a penny, in for a pound, too. My boss will never forgive me if I let this chance go." Resolutely not thinking about the chance of getting a piece of real news that might be resold to the daily papers, Parris made up his mind.

Maria stood like a statue, her back to him and the passenger door open, her hand holding the handle.

"Fine," he agreed. "Your car, your rules." He walked past her, and stopped with one foot in the car, and one foot on the pavement. "You are sure?" he asked Maria. Briefly, she inclined her head.

Parris sat down on the front passenger seat, and at once, Maria closed the car door firmly. Then she walked, still with that slow but purposeful; stride, around the back of the car to the driver's door. She opened the door and got into the car rather clumsily. Her skirt dragged up her left leg as she slid awkwardly onto the seat, and Parris suspected that she was wearing no underwear. That made him feel rather uncomfortable, and he half turned to look at Maria whilst leaning back against his door. Maria did not look at him at all. She leant forward and fumbled with the keys, before finally pushing the main key into the car ignition, and starting the engine.

"Seatbelt," she finally spoke. Her voice was hoarse, the word forced through her throat as if speaking was unfamiliar to her.

Parris wondered how he was going to interview someone who clearly spoke very little, but decided that he could at least get her to nod or shake her head as he asked questions, and a little creative licence would do the rest of the job. He twisted to his left, and grabbed the seat belt. Pulling the belt across his body, he lifted the camera on its strap so that it lay on top of the seat belt. Maria's left hand, holding the buckle of her seat belt, made a couple of inaccurate jabs at the fastener. Parris reached out and helped her. He looked up in surprise: she had not even looked down. Her hand felt cool under his, and she made no effort to pull her hand away. Whilst her hand looked quite flabby, he was surprised by the unexpected strength he could feel as he pulled her hand away from the buckle of the belt.

"Where are we going?" asked Parris.

Maria did not reply, but turned on the right hand indicator. Then she put her foot on the brake pedal, and pulled the gear lever down to the 'Drive' position. Parris was mildly surprised to find that the small hatchback had an automatic gearbox. With a sudden roar as the accelerator was pressed hard, Maria pulled away from the kerb. Parris closed his eyes as she narrowly missed hitting the police car.

"Wow, you got a bit close, there!" he said, again leaning against the car door.

Still looking straight ahead, Maria reached to her door and operated the central locking mechanism. Parris assumed that this was so that the car door could not open unexpectedly, but it still made him a little uncomfortable.

"Do you mind if I take another picture? This time a close up?" he asked as Maria drove inexpertly through the town traffic. She did not reply.

Parris looked out of the window as she drove, and tried to memorise the route she was taking. After all, he would need to return later to get his own car, and he was beginning to think that he did not want to return in the car with Maria. Her progress through the late afternoon traffic was marked by the noise of horns blaring as other drivers expressed their anger at her driving skills and technique.

"Go on, just one whilst we drive?" asked Parris, who was feeling unnerved by the silence inside the car. Maria did not reply, so he slipped the lens cap from the camera and turned it towards her face.

Maria immediately reacted. Still expressionless, she reached across with her left hand, and pushed the camera away from her face, taking a firm grip on the body of the camera and covering the lens with her fingers.

"Ow!" yelled Parris loudly, as she tugged sharply on the camera. He ducked his head, and the strap was pulled roughly across his head until it came free. Maria tossed the camera onto the back seat, without looking at him.

"You cow, that's an expensive piece of kit!" objected Parris.

Maria looked at him, and then looked back at the road. Her face was still expressionless, and the sunglasses concealed her eyes. She removed her left hand from the steering wheel, and took Parris' right hand in her own. She placed his hand high on her thigh and pulled up her skirt from below his hand. Parris' suspicions about her lack of clothing grew stronger, but his gaze was drawn away as she indicated left and turned inexpertly into the grounds of an old and abandoned factory.

The brick walls had faded in colour. Many of the windows in the factory were broken, and the rain guttering had sagged or broken. The paint on the window frames and doors was faded and peeling or gone entirely. Glass lay around the bottom of the buildings, together with blown leaves and small mounds of rubbish. Parris could see that one or two of the wooden doors in the old mill had been broken open. An elderly sign warned of a security presence and guard dogs, but clearly both were, like the owners and the workers in the factory, long gone.

Parris started to ask why she had chosen to come here but suddenly decided that Maria had her own agenda in mind. He did not remove his hand from her thigh and his pulse started to beat faster.

The car slid on a patch of loose gravel and Parris' attention was distracted from Maria's naked leg. The thigh muscle twitched under his hand, and his cheeks flushed. Looking around he could see that Maria was stopping the car in the rear courtyard of the factory. Dust from the tyres rose up around the car, obscuring his view of the buildings. Maria reached down and unclipped her seatbelt. The belt wound itself back, the silver buckle sliding slowly across her body. Parris followed it with his eyes, and reaching down, he too released his seat belt.

Maria released the back support of her seat, and allowed herself to slowly lean backwards, her hands now raised above her head. Still she was completely without expression, inscrutable behind the mirrored sunglasses. Parris released the back of his seat too and scrabbled at his clothing. He turned back towards Maria, and wriggled until he was lying partly on top of her. Her hands reached out for him, and clumsily he started to respond. But his left hand managed to knock her sunglasses from her face.

Parris froze, and then opened his mouth to scream and scream and scream at the sight of her eyes. They were suffused with red, the whites of the eyes gone and the pupils a mere black slit in the fiery crimson glow. Her hands gripped him tightly, pulling him towards her: and for the first time since Andy Parris had got into her car. Maria smiled.

Chapter Eight

Jane stood impassively at the front door of the Balsam's and watched it close behind Sheila Balsam, leaving her - she supposed - alone in the house except for a cleaner who would be leaving shortly. Her hand rested on the statuette of the unicorn, and after a heartbeat she looked closely at it.

"I thought you were a lighter colour than that?" she asked the statuette, and then giggled at the thought that she might actually get an answer. Remembering that her earlier experience in the house had been uncomfortable, she stopped giggling. Unbidden, as she looked at the unicorn, memories of events that now made her feel ashamed arose and demanded her attention. He distress as her husband left her for another woman, and the wild night of clubbing where she had taken two boys home with her. She blushed again, this time in self reproach: then a scandalous thought came to her: what if her behaviour had not been wrong, but right? What if her instinct to wash away the humiliation in that way had been the best possible response, that her lust and anger were matters for pride not regret? Revulsion at those strange feelings swept through her, and they vanished.

Trying to clear her mind of the unwelcome vision, Jane decided that since she had - and she was still not entirely sure why - agreed to house sit for the expected delivery (whatever it was to be), she might as well have a cup of tea whilst she waited.

First she walked into the living room, and looked around. The seat near the front window would do her very well, she thought. Plus there were some paperback books stacked on the floor near the window, so she would be able to find a way to occupy the time of waiting for the delivery and provide a suddenly welcome distraction.

Jane took off her jacket, and draped it over the arm of the nearest chair. Her handbag she dropped onto the same chair, before examining the rest of the living room with curiosity. The chairs were worn, but comfortable. The sofa was hidden under various rugs and throws, but was clearly well used. The scatter cushions were in fact scattered across the furniture, with one or two lying on the floor near the fireplace. A mug, half full of cold coffee, stood on a side table. The coffee table in the middle of the room was bare, except for some coasters and a half open book that lay face down on the table. Jane looked at the cover: it was a Mills and Boon book, and did not appeal to her tastes.

She left the living room, leaving the door open behind her, and walked into the kitchen. She looked round the empty room, and remembering her experience that morning felt the first hint of an unease or tension in the atmosphere around her. Jane walked over to the worktop and picked up the kettle. She turned to the sink to fill the kettle, and dropped it in surprise. The kettle hit the enamel sink with a loud clattering sound. Jane hunched her shoulders and stepped back from the sink, her eyes not leaving the window.

"I'm sure that I saw something!" she exclaimed aloud. "The same face as before!"

Breathing in, and holding her breath she summoned up her courage, and spun suddenly around on one heel to see if the image that had alarmed - no either frightened, or terrified - her was behind her in the kitchen.

Her relief that the kitchen was still empty and that she was alone, was tangible and she released her held-in breath with a rush. She looked back at the kitchen window, the impression of a face she had seen was gone, and all she could see was the view down the back garden.

"How stupid am I?" she said aloud. The sound of her own voice was thin and weak in the oppressive atmosphere of the kitchen, but still made her feel better. Jane turned back to the sink and picked up the kettle she had dropped. She turned it over and looked at it, trying to see if the kettle had been damaged when she dropped it. Apart from a small chip in the colouring on the side of the kettle, she could see no damage so she filled the kettle from the tap. This took a little longer than it might, as her hand shook every time that her eyes glanced towards the kitchen window. She did her best to fill the kettle with her eyes averted and downcast.

At last she felt that there must be enough water in the kettle. Steeling her nerves she looked at the tap and saw that the kettle was in fact overflowing with water. She quickly turned off the tap, and allowed some more water to flow out of the kettle. The electric base of the kettle lay to her right, and with a rush of relief she turned away from the window and the sink and placed the kettle on the base. She flicked the switch and stepped back wards slightly, before putting both her hands on the worktop and bowing her head.

"Why did I agree to stay in this house?" she asked herself.

"Why? Why?" She repeated "Why? Why?" more loudly, and the echo ran from the kitchen into the hall. Jane shivered. "I'll be jumping at shadows at this rate," she said to herself. Then she laughed nervously, a forced and harsh sound and she found herself looking into the corners of the kitchen to seek out the shadows for a threat or a menace.

The kettle boiled and whistled, a shrill sound that startled her. Jane opened various wall cupboards, deliberately slamming each door closed so that the sound filled the kitchen. At last she found both coffee and mugs, and placed each down on the worktop, rather too loudly. She spooned coffee into the mug, and left the jar out on the worktop. She splashed boiling water into the mug, and looked around for the fridge.

"Damn" Jane muttered. "It's one of those hidden behind an ordinary cupboard door."

She started opening doors, and banging them closed in annoyance and frustration as she failed to find the fridge and the milk. She passed by the doors underneath the sink and the next cupboard below the worktop was the last : but it held only crockery. Jane cursed to herself.

"Maybe it's that tall cupboard at the end?" she wondered. She reached out to the handle on the door of the tall cupboard, but then pulled back and turned away.

"The blasted coffee will be cold by the time that I find the milk," she told herself. Jane walked back to the kettle and picked it up. She squinted at the water level indicator, and told herself that there was enough water in the kettle for a second mug. She turned on the kettle, and picked up the mug full of black coffee.

"Waste, I know," she said and poured the coffee out into the sink. Jane put the mug back down on the worktop, and spooned more coffee powder into it from the jar. Then she walked back across the kitchen to the tall larder cupboard door, and opened it wide. Her hand flew from the handle to her mouth, and she staggered backwards. The door had opened to reveal the entrance to the cellar. There at the top of the steps stood Maria, her clothes and hair untidy.

SOCO officers receive quite extensive training in many things, but all of that is usually unnecessary when it comes to recognising a dead body and Jane's admittedly limited experience in the job still allowed her to realise immediately that she faced a dead body, and she relaxed slightly, assuming that it had been propped up or supported in some way. Once again the house had become a crime scene, she thought.

"I must call this in," she said, getting control of her riotous emotions and trying hard to become professional. Her heart rate began to fall, and she took several deep breaths to help calm her nerves.

All this effort was wasted when Maria's body twitched. Jane looked her up and down, and tried and tried and tried unsuccessfully to scream as she saw that Maria's eyes were glowing crimson red. Jane opened her mouth and did scream, loudly and without pause as Maria walked out of what Jane had taken to be a cupboard and came towards her across the kitchen. With no thought of escape, only of terror, Jane backed away until the worktop in the corner of the kitchen stopped her going further. She sank into a crouch with a small mew of horror as Maria loomed above her and the afternoon light cast shadows around her.

Nothing happened.

Jane crouched down, hardly breathing, waiting to be attacked. She had watched many horror movies and images from them flashed across her mind, memories of gruesome and awful deaths. She had no doubt that was what awaited her any moment, and the anticipation became unbearable. Finally, as Maria loomed above her but made no move to attack her, she moved herself. She pushed her right leg out to one side, and then leant after it, moving with exquisite care. Heartbeats passed in between each movement. She pushed away with her left leg, and her body came free from Maria's shadow. Hope started to blossom in her that she might, after all, escape. Slowly, so slowly, she pulled her left leg away from the still figure. Now she was entirely to one side. On all fours, whimpering with a mixture of relief and terror, she scuttled on all fours across the kitchen, away, away from the horror that was now behind her.

Breathing in ragged bursts, Jane was not surprised to find that she was weeping as she pushed herself unsteadily to her feet. A rapid glance behind her showed that, miraculously, the awful apparition had not moved from the corner and she had a chance of freedom. She started to run for the front door that represented light, freedom and safety. She grabbed at the door frame as she ran into the hall, turned towards the front door and escape: and stopped short.

There at the door stood the statuette of the unicorn, facing towards her. As she watched, the dark shadow behind the unicorn grew on the wall, rose up and became defined. The horn rose from his brow as the shadowman stepped away from the wall.

Jane put her hand to her mouth. Rooted to the spot on which she stood, she felt unable to move. The shadows twisted. Now she could see a hard, muscular, male body, with long arms. The face became more shaped, the horn now a thing of wonder. Two eyes opened with a red glow that also lit the mouth, now opened in a triumphant, leering smile.

Slowly the shadowman stepped forward towards Jane. She took a pace backwards, and realised that someone was behind her. Slowly she looked over her shoulder, and there stood Maria, so close that they were almost touching. The shadowman came close, and held out his hand in invitation, rather than threat.

"What do you want of me?" asked Jane, in a small, tremulous voice.

A second hand was extended towards her, perhaps in supplication.

"What do you want?" Jane's voice rose, a hint of hysteria now in the tone.

The horn dipped towards her.

"No. NO!"

Jane held out her hands, palms upturned, a gesture of rejection and denial. The shadow's hands reached towards her, and she tried to move backwards. The stocky body behind her was immobile, solid as a rock and she tried to push herself sideways, away. An unnaturally firm hand pushed her in the middle of her back, forcing her forward and into the shadowman's welcoming embrace. The shadow enclosed and enfolded her, and Jane finally looked up into the glowing, crimson eyes and was lost. As the shadows took her into the living room, Maria walked slowly down the hall to the front door, which she opened. Closing it behind her, she walked down the garden path.

*

Sheila Balsam sat at the interview table, and treated first Inspector Peake and then Sergeant Wilson to a long stare. A woman police officer stood silently beside the door of the interview room, but Sheila ignored her.

"Inspector, I feel that you are wasting my time," Sheila said in a crisp tone.

She turned to look at Sergeant Wilson. "And you do not need to give me that sort of stare, sergeant."

"I'm sorry?" asked Wilson.

"Miss Balsam," said Inspector Peake, ignoring that exchange, "you know these enquiries are both important and urgent."

"Inspector, my poor mother is dead and lying in the morgue. I rather doubt that she feels any sense of urgency or importance."

Peake leant forward across the table. "What about you though, Miss Balsam? Are you not in a hurry to have your mother's killer found and brought to justice?"

Sheila returned his look. "Inspector Peake, I am many things. I am a bit too quiet, easily cowed, and my mother was a very dominant person. But I am not a hypocrite. I cannot in honesty tell you that I am not better off for my mother's passing."

"Miss Balsam, she was killed," Wilson pointed out.

"We all get to die sometime, somehow, sergeant."

"You are not bothered that she was murdered, then?" asked Peake, carefully.

"Inspector, I would have much preferred my mother to die a natural, peaceful death in her own bed. Of course I would. But it is a fact that she is gone now, isn't it?"

"Yes," agreed Wilson, eyeing Miss Balsam with growing interest.

"So what am I doing here?"

"Miss Balsam, it is my job to find who killed your mother."

Sheila Balsam shrugged.

"Are you not at least interested in knowing the truth?" asked Sergeant Wilson.

"Sergeant, the fact is that my mother is on a slab in the hospital, five miles up the road from here. That is the only truth I need to know."

"Are you sorry that she is dead?" asked Peake.

"Send not to ask for whom the bell tolls, Inspector?"

"What?" Wilson did not recognise the quotation or understand the point.

Peake however did. "Miss Balsam, your mother was hardly a stranger to you, was she? You were involved with her. She was your mother!"

"Correct, Inspector, she was." Sheila placed a subtle emphasis on the word 'was', and both Peake and Wilson noticed.

"So, your relationship with your mother was not the best?" asked Peake.

"You told me that your job is to find out how she died?" asked Sheila.

"Could you please answer the question, Miss Balsam?" asked Inspector Peake.

"How does my relationship with my mother help you?" asked Sheila. Then a thought occurred to her. "Am I a suspect? Do you think that I killed my own mother?"

"Miss Balsam, we have to eliminate you from the enquiry so that we can move on," Sergeant Wilson said diplomatically.

"But that's not what you are thinking is it?"

Inspector Peake leant back in his chair. "Miss Balsam, we have to run through all the possibilities. That's our job, you understand."

"And I am a possibility?"

"Miss Balsam," said Sergeant Wilson, "family members are

always a possibility, sadly."

"And I, of course, am the only family member."

"Well, yes. So, Miss Balsam, what was your relationship with your mother like?"

"Quite normal between a young woman and a domineering mother when they live together, I should think."

Inspector Peake made a brief note on his pad. "Can we run through the day before your mother died please?"

"What would you like to know?" asked Sheila.

"Tell me what you did that day, please."

"Let me see, I went to work as normal, came home as normal, cooked as normal..." Sheila shrugged. "It was just a day like any other."

"Do you know what your mother did?"

"Some knitting maybe, Inspector? Perhaps she pottered about in the garden or read a book. It was a nice day, wasn't it? Perhaps she took a book outside into the sunshine."

"Did you not ask her what she did with her day?" asked Sergeant Wilson.

"Probably she told me, Sergeant. That doesn't mean that I listened does it? She didn't go out very often, so one day was much like another for her."

"Had she many friends?" asked Inspector Peake.

"My mother? Who would be friends with her?"

Both Peake and Wilson remained quiet and watched Sheila until she felt compelled by the silence to add to the comment.

"My mother tended to drive people away by being too bossy and overbearing, Inspector. So no, she had very few friends. And they mostly live at some distance."

"She didn't drive you away?"

"Sergeant, she was my mother. I didn't have to like her, just to put up with her. Now I don't have to, do I?"

"Miss Balsam, did anything happen on that day which made you concerned for your mother's safety at all?"

"Hardly, Inspector. If I had been concerned, then I would not have gone to bed as early as I did."

"Earlier than usual?" asked Wilson.

"Yes, sergeant. And no, before you ask, there are no witnesses to that. You will just have to take my word for it."

"We did find traces of soil in the hall," said Peake, after looking at his notes.

"Yes. I knocked over a plant pot. Not an earth shattering event, Inspector. Except for the plant, obviously."

Peake sighed very heavily. "So, on the day that you found your mother, Miss Balsam…"

"Yes?"

"Can you just take us through the events again?"

"I've already given you two statements on the day, about that day, Inspector. Isn't that enough for you?"

"Well we do find that sometimes people remember extra little details, Miss Balsam. And sometimes those details can make all the difference."

"Really. Well, I find that I have nothing else to add to my earlier statements, Inspector."

Peake and Wilson exchanged looks. Sheila Balsam stood up.

"If you don't mind, I'd rather like to go home now, Inspector. Do I get transport?"

"I have not terminated the interview, Miss Balsam."

"Maybe, but I have. And since I am not under arrest - unsurprising really as I have committed no offence - I am choosing to leave."

Peake and Wilson exchanged looks again, and Peake nodded. "That is your right, Miss Balsam. As you say, you have not been detained," agreed Peake.

Wilson leant across the table towards the recording machine. "Interview terminated at..." he paused to check his watch. "Four-thirty pm," he finished. He turned the tape recorder off and removed both cassette tapes.

Sheila Balsam cast him an amused look. "Whatever are you doing, sergeant?"

"Procedure, Miss." Wilson bagged and sealed both tapes, labelled them and offered one tape to her.

Sheila Balsam laughed at him. "Whatever am I supposed to do with that?"

"It is your record of the interview, Miss," replied Wilson.

"I hardly think that I am going to need one." Sheila Balsam turned to look Peake directly in the eyes. "Inspector, I did not kill my mother. I do not know who did. I wish you luck in your endeavours, but would prefer not to be bothered again."

She walked at the door to the interview room and stared at the woman police officer who guarded the door. The latter looked at Inspector Peake for guidance: Peake nodded, and the door was opened. Sheila swept out of the interview room.

*

The constable in the marked police car that was parked outside the Balsam house awoke from his drowse with a start. A large delivery van had just arrived and parked behind him very quietly. He climbed out of the patrol car and walked up to the driver's door of the delivery van. He looked down the side of the van, but it was unmarked and no signs adorned the panels of the anonymous van.

"Can I help you, officer?" asked the driver. His face was shadowed by his large baseball cap, and the constable could see little more than a beard and gleaming eyes.

"There was an incident here recently, and I'm just making sure that all visitors are bona fide."

The driver shrugged. "I'm just delivering an order, mate. Here's my delivery note." He put his left hand out, and his companion slapped a clipboard into it. The driver pushed it out of the window at the constable, who took it and looked briefly at the paper on the board.

"Looks legit," agreed the constable. "Sorry to bother you, lads. But you know how it is."

The driver took back the clipboard, and passed it to his companion. Then he opened his door, and jumped out onto the road, in front of the constable. The policeman looked up at the dark, saturnine face of the driver, who smiled at him with a flash of white teeth. The constable nodded and walked back to the patrol car.

The other occupant of the van jumped out of the vehicle and walked around to the back of the van. He unlocked the double doors with a special key, and opened the doors wide. The driver watched the policeman get back inside the patrol car before he moved away from his door. When the door of the police car was safely closed, he joined his colleague at the rear of the van.

The inside of the large van was dark, but the delivery men seemed to have no trouble seeing inside. A large packet of papers was tied to the first object. The driver took the packet of papers and the clipboard still held by his assistant, and walked down the path to the front door of the Balsam's house. He knocked hard on the door. Jane opened the door: silently he held out the clipboard with one hand and the packet of papers with the other. Without speaking, Jane took the pen that was held on the clipboard with a piece of string and signed the bottom of the delivery note. She took the envelope full of papers with the other hand, and handed back the clipboard. The delivery man walked back to the van.

He nodded to his colleague, and they both reached into the van. Each pulled out an ornately carved wooden chair, holding it carefully with both hands. They walked slowly in procession down the drive to the house. Jane held the front door open, and the delivery men vanished inside. After a brief time they reappeared and walked back to the van. Again they reached into the back of the van, and each took out a carved chair identical to the first pair.

Again they walked slowly down the drive and vanished into the house. Once more there was a stillness around the front door before they returned. The two men walked slowly to the delivery van. This time the driver climbed into the back of the van, and his assistant reached as far into the van as he could. Slowly he stood upright, holding the legs of a fifth chair. He slowly walked backwards as the driver emerged from the depths of the van holding the carved and ornate back of the fifth chair. Carefully, so that the wood touched nothing of the delivery van, he climbed out. This chair was twice the size of the other chairs: a Master's chair, perhaps a Throne. It was also very heavy and the two delivery men took especial pains and care with the chair as they manoeuvred it down the drive and into the house. This time the front door closed behind them, and it was some time before they came back out.

The delivery men finally came back out and walked back to the delivery van in silence. They climbed into the respective sides of the cab and drove away without fuss.

*

Jane again closed the front door, and stood facing it. Slowly she lifted her right hand, and placed it - without needing to look - upon the unicorn statuette. Her eyes glowed a deep crimson for just an instant, then the colour faded and washed away. Turning, Jane blinked and walked away from the front door.

Her steps were slow and stately, her carriage firm and erect as she paced down the length of the hall. With a conscious effort she pulled back her shoulders and kept her head high. At the end of the hall she turned into the kitchen and without hesitation opened the cupboard door that hid the concealed entrance to the cellar. The pull cord for the light hung to her right, but she ignored it, and walked down the stone steps without a pause.

The cellar had changed. Whilst the racks of tools and the workbench remained in place, the floor had been freshly swept clear of dust. The chalk circle had been freshly inscribed in a perfect ring and certain mystical signs had been drawn on the floor at the cardinal points of the circle. The five carved chairs had been arranged around the circle. Yet they were not perfectly equidistant: a small gap to each side of the Master Chair gave it an air of prominence. In the space between each chair was placed an ornate candle stand. Each stand bore a tall black candle, and each candle was lit. A thin plume of dark smoke rose from the melting wax, and a heady, musky scent filled the air.

At the bottom of the steps into the cellar Jane paused. She looked at each chair in turn before slowly walking around the circle anti clockwise, breathing in the dark perfume. She walked around the circle three times, and at the completion of the third circuit she stopped behind one chair. She touched the back of the chair, her hand caressing the ornate carvings. A sense of age, of archaic times filled her as did a recognition that she was not the first to complete the coming ritual, but one of a long line - a line without number or end stretching back into primeval times - and that knowledge both frightened and comforted her.

Taking great care not to step upon the chalk markings, Jane stepped over the lines and entered the circle. At once the candles flared, the flames flickering and fluttering, sending shadows racing around the cellar. The perfume grew stronger, and Jane turned to face the empty Master Chair. Slowly, deliberately she moved until she stood within the circle but directly before the Chair. The candles fluttered again, and the chair was no longer empty. The shadowman sat there, the horn rising from his noble brow, his eyes a deep crimson with slitted pupils of jet. Jane looked at him, examined the hard, masculine body and the strong limbs that gripped the ornate and raised arms of the chair.

The shadowman dipped his head in acknowledgement of her, and Jane took a single pace backwards, towards the very centre of the circle. The chalk markings began to glow, infused by an eldritch golden light.

Jane raised both her hands to her throat, then slowly she began to unbutton her blouse. As each button was released, a little more of her body was revealed to the impassive gaze of the shadowman. When she reached the final button, Jane allowed her blouse to hang loose and open for a moment before she rolled her shoulders and slipped the blouse down the length of her body. It fell loose from her arms and collapsed around her ankles. Her eyes remained on the shadowman as he now gained shape and definition.

Her hands now reached behind her, rising up the curve of her back until they reached the fastenings of her remaining covering. Her fingers slipped behind the strap of her bra, and with a practised flick she undid the clips. Slowly she brought the wide straps around her sides and then released them. Crossing her arms over her chest she reached for the straps that lay over each shoulder, and pulled them away. Finally she dropped the bra at her feet, her gaze riveted on the shadowman as he sat motionless, waiting, watching.

The waistband of Jane's skirt was held in place with a button and a short zipper. First she released the button, and then she slowly slid the zip down to its end and let go of the fabric. The skirt dropped to the floor and she stood naked before the shadowman. Jane took a pace backwards, free of the material around her feet and sank to her knees, her back arched and her body displayed.

The shadowman dipped the horn rising from his brow in appreciation three times, then he stood. He stepped into the circle and knelt down before her, at a small distance. His head bowed, then the horn thrust into Jane's body just below the left breast, piercing the heart.

Jane, transfixed, gave a low moan. The tableau froze, a still moment in time. Then the shadowman drew back, and raised his head. A thin trickle of blood ran down from the sharp tip of the horn, and then was absorbed. A second line of blood ran down from the pierced hole in Jane's chest, down towards her navel. She was so still that she might have been a statue.

Slowly the shadowman extended an arm, and with one finger he reached out and wiped away the blood. He raised that finger to his lips and licked it with appreciation and enjoyment. The wound in Jane's chest closed.

Jane moved. She lay back down upon the stone floor and opened her arms, careful not to touch the golden glow from the chalk circle. Her legs moved apart, and the shadowman leant forward. His hands landed on either side of her, and Jane smiled at the strength in the biceps, at the hard and muscular body now raised above her and at the chiselled features now so clear to her, the close cropped but curled hair almost hiding the pointed ears, and the gleaming white teeth. The arms bent and the shadowman lowered himself towards her.

At that moment, the single dim light bulb lit, casting a dim but fresh light upon the scene. A single scream rang out, choked into a silence. Sheila Balsam stood at the top of the stone steps, the door to the kitchen open behind her and her right hand raised on the pull cord of the light switch.

Sheila froze for a long moment, taking in all the details of the nightmare scene below her, and then she turned and fled, the kitchen door slamming closed behind her. The light bulb swung from the vibration of the slamming door, and the disturbed air made the candles flicker and gutter. Jane gasped, but the shadowman was gone.

Chapter Nine

Sheila Balsam walked confidently away from the interview room in the police station, the woman police officer who had been present at her interview hurrying after her.

"Miss Balsam!" called the officer.

"Yes?" replied Sheila, without breaking her stride.

"You cannot just walk out of a police station, you know!"

"Really? I am not being detained, so I rather think that I can!"

The constable caught up with Sheila, and matched strides with her. "Well, you will find it a bit easier if I am with you."

Sheila suddenly laughed. "Yes, I suppose that I will, thank you."

"Inspector Peake has told me to give you a lift home."

"That's very kind of you," Sheila told her, "but I don't think it is necessary."

"It's no trouble."

"I'm sure. But if you don't mind, I'd rather make my own way home."

They reached the stairs, and the constable pointed downwards. Sheila at once set off.

At the bottom of the stairs, Sheila looked at the heavily secured doors.

"You were quite right to see me out, and I'm sorry if I was abrupt," she told the constable.

"No apology needed, Miss Balsam." The constable went to the security desk, and exchanged a few words with the sergeant there. Then she walked back to Sheila.

"Here is a card with Inspector Peake's telephone number. If anything occurs to you, or you remember anything suddenly, will you please call?"

"Yes of course I will," lied Sheila.

The constable nodded to the desk sergeant, and the doors gave first a loud buzz and then a click: the universal sign that secure doors had just been unlocked. Sheila pushed hard at one door, and it opened. She walked firmly out of the police station and onto the busy road. A hundred yards down the road lay a bus stop, and Sheila walked over and checked the time table. Unprepared to wait as long as was required, she turned her attention to the traffic, and waited for a taxi.

Before too long a cab came along, and was prepared to stop when hailed. "I'm not really sure why I'm doing this," said the taxi driver as Sheila opened the rear door of the taxi. "I'm not supposed to!"

"Well I am not about to complain to anyone about you, so don't worry," replied Sheila.

"Where do you want to go, miss?"

"As far away as I can get," replied Sheila, leaning back in the seat and closing her eyes.

"I mean right now?"

Still with her eyes closed, Sheila gave the driver her address and her input the details into his Satnav before pulling out into the traffic.

"Isn't that where the murder happened?" asked the driver.

"Yes. But don't ask me about it or you'll be the next victim."

The driver started to laugh, caught sight of Sheila's face in his rear view mirror and stopped laughing abruptly. "Right," he said and didn't speak again until he drew up at the Balsam house.

"That will be six pounds fifty, please," he asked after he had parked and checked the meter.

Sheila gave him a very long, considered look.

"Six pounds fifty," repeated the driver.

"Would you consider something else instead?" asked Sheila.

"Lady, I get that all the time."

"And what do you say to these ladies, mister taxi driver?"

"The same as I'll say to you. I'm happily married, and I'll just take the fare please."

"You say that to them all?" asked Sheila, peering closely at the driver.

"Yes."

"You know, I see that you do, don't you? Well, well, who would have thought it?" Sheila opened her handbag and took out a ten pound note. "Keep the change."

"You sure, miss?"

"Quite sure. Thank you for the lift."

Sheila opened the back door of the taxi, climbed out and closed the door without slamming it. Mildly surprised by this, the taxi driver lost no time in making his getaway. Ignoring the constable in the marked police patrol car, Sheila walked down the drive to the front door. When it did not open for her at her approach she took her house keys from her handbag and opened the door.

The light was now diminishing, and the hall was full of shadows. Sheila immediately put out her hand and caressed the statuette, then withdrew her hand with a puzzled expression. She had expected to feel a jolt of emotion, a feeling of power suppressed and denied from the unicorn, but the figurine felt blank and empty.

Sheila felt both relieved and cheated, then concerned. Never before had she failed to feel a range of complex and conflicting thoughts upon touching the unicorn, and could not understand why this time was so different. She walked slowly down the hall and into the kitchen.

On the kitchen table lay a thick packet of papers, addressed to her. Sheila opened the envelope and looked at the contents. First was a simple delivery note, detailing her address and contact details. The exact contents of the delivery were not described beyond 'five pieces of antique furniture as arranged, to be positioned as required'. The other sheets were clearly very old, and the paper was thick and creamy yet fragile. Perhaps, thought Sheila, ancient parchment? Gingerly she turned some of the sheets. The pages were covered in words written in a crabbed hand, in fading black ink. In places the lettering had turned brown through age. Various drawings and inscriptions were mixed in amongst the text. Closing the sheets, she noticed the names 'Solomon' 'Agrippa' and 'Honorious' all of which were vaguely familiar to her, then she returned the pages to the dining table.

A small noise startled her. "The house is empty - isn't it?" she said aloud. Then slowly her gaze was drawn to the closed door that led to the cellar. Unwillingly she walked to the door. She had to draw several deep breaths before she opened the door. The pull cord for the light switch hung immediately beside her right hand, and without thinking, by force of habit, she reached out and pulled the cord. The weak electric light added to the glow from the candles below.

Sheila caught her breath, a small sound of disbelief. Black candles were placed between the ornate wooden chairs around the glowing golden circle on the cellar floor. The smoke rising from the wicks held a bitter, acrid tang and drawn towards the open door it stung her eyes. Within the circle, Jane writhed naked below the so very solid figure of the shadowman. Sheila screamed. She stepped backwards and slammed the door on the sight, shutting it from her vision if not from her memory. She ran. She ran from the kitchen, along the hall, and dragged the front door wide open, letting in a blast of cold fresh air into the close atmosphere.

The unicorn seemed to shimmer, and turned to face the front door. "Sheila, Sheila..."

Sheila heard the seductive voice call her name, but at that moment it held no power over her.

"No!" she gasped. "No!"

"Come!" the voice commanded her, the tone overladen with both power and authority.

Used to obeying without question such a voice when employed by her mother, Sheila stopped on the threshold.

"Come! Obey!" the voice in Sheila's head commanded again.

Sheila took a single step backwards. The compulsion to obey, to submit, to comply was momentarily overwhelming. Then her new found rejection of such tyranny came to the fore: "NO!" she shouted, and strode over the threshold of her house, out onto the path. At once the compulsion to surrender fell away, and Sheila started to sob. Escape was now her primary goal and she set off towards the police patrol car.

"No!" she gasped again. The garden gate opened, and there stood Maria, known to Sheila to be quite dead. With no expression upon her face, Maria started down the garden path towards her. She did not need to look to feel the shadow rising at her back, reaching out for her. With another sob, Sheila took the only possible route left to her. She ran across the grass, her shoes slipping, and jumped over the small fence between the two gardens. A moment later she was hammering frantically upon Mister Jones' front door.

The door opened, and with out a word Sheila pushed the astonished Mister Jones back down his own hallway, followed him inside and kicked the front door shut against the terrors of the night, now abroad and dangerous in the daylight.

*

I was watching the early evening news program on TV when I was disturbed by a violent hammering on my front door.

"Now what?" I asked myself. In fact I was not displeased to have an excuse to leave the news. As always it was sufficiently disturbing, even at that early time, to make me despair for the whole race of humanity. It seemed to me that the most ancient and terrible of demons could have learned a new trick or two for their trade from watching the international news.

The frantic hammering on the door continued, and I walked down the hall and threw open the front door. There stood a highly agitated Sheila Balsam, and before I could speak she pushed me hard in the chest with one hand. I staggered backwards, and she jumped inside the house after me, kicked my door closed so hard that the entire house shook, and then collapsed against me. I grabbed hold of her to stop her falling to the floor.

"Sheila? Sheila? Whatever is the matter? Are you all right?"

"I am now that I'm here," she replied, and held onto me in a way I found quite disturbing.

A moment later there was another solid knock on my door.

"Don't answer that!" said Sheila, holding me more tightly still.

"But?" I started to ask.

"If you value your life, do NOT open that door!" Sheila said.

"Who is it?" I asked.

"It is my cleaner, Maria."

"Well, why shouldn't I answer it then?"

"Because she is dead," replied Sheila dramatically.

I stepped backwards, away from the door as the heavy knock came again. Since she was holding me so tightly, Sheila naturally followed and then wanted to keep going. Slowly I walked backwards into the living room, her head pressed against my chest and her arms tight around me.

"Dead?" I asked slowly. "How do you know?"

"I put her body in my cellar," replied Sheila.

I tried to pull away a little at that remark, but Sheila kept her grip on me.

"Now I'm trying to get away, and they are coming for me!" she said, somewhat hysterically.

The word 'they' I found a little disturbing. The sound of knocking at the front door stopped, and Sheila relaxed a little. I became considerably more tense as I could see the cleaner clearly through the front window, staring at us as we stood beside the fireplace. I tried to prise Sheila's hands from my back, but failed. I stared at the cleaner, who looked impassively at us through the window.

"Are all your doors locked?" asked Sheila.

"Not the back door, no. But this is my home, Sheila."

"So?" she asked.

"So nothing can come in here without my express invitation."

Now Sheila let go of me, and straightened up. "How can you be sure?"

I took her hands. "Trust me on this. It might surprise you, but I have a little experience and knowledge here."

Sheila dropped my left hand, her right hand flew to her mouth, and her eyes opened wide in horror. "You are not involved with - them - with *him* - are you?"

"No. Whoever you are talking about, I can assure you that I am not."

"Mister Jones, we are still in danger then. You see..." her voice trailed away.

"What? I asked urgently.

"The bedroom I used here, with the hole in the wall..."

"What?"

"I invited - *him* - through into that room." Her head turned to look at the ceiling.

"That's of no consequence," I told her. "I've stopped up that

175

hole. I haven't repaired it properly, but I have blocked it."

There was a knock on the front door again. Moments later there came another knock on the back door, and Sheila started shaking again.

"Have you got any windows open?" she asked.

I shook my head reassuringly. "The evening air was getting a chill, so I closed them before the news came on the TV."

Sheila relaxed again.

"Who is at the back door?" I asked her.

"Probably a policewoman," she replied.

I was startled. "Surely I should answer that then?"

"Not unless you want to kill us both," she told me. Sheila started to get a grip on herself. "Mister Jones, I owe you an explanation and the whole story."

I pursed my lips. "That seems about fair. You run in here, and then tell me that my house is surrounded by - what, zombies? An explanation seems reasonable."

"I don't know if they are zombies. But is there any way that we can get away from here?"

"Do they talk?" I asked.

Sheila shuddered. "*He* does. Inside my head. The other two, I don't know."

I nodded, and guided Sheila to the sofa. "Sit down," I told her gently.

"Where are you going?" she asked, an undertone of panic in her voice.

"I'm going to see who is at the back door." I held up my hand as she started from the couch. "Promise that I shan't talk to them or open the door. But the telephone is in the kitchen, and I think we need to call for help."

With that I walked first to the front window. Immediately the cleaner appeared at the other side of the glass, staring right into my eyes. I looked at her, and banished any doubts about Sheila's sanity. It was only too easy to believe that I was looking at a walking dead body. I closed the curtains firmly, to shut out the sight, and Sheila relaxed a little.

"I'm only going to get the telephone," I said again in reassurance.

Sheila nodded then, so I left the living room, walked across the darkening hall and into the kitchen. Immediately there was another knock on the back door. Naturally I looked to see who it was, and was quite taken aback to see a completely naked girl - well, very obviously a fully grown woman - there, with one hand raised to the glass. On seeing me, she smiled, and slowly ran her hands up and down her body in a clear invitation. She beckoned, and pointed to the door, before repeating the gesture. Then she placed her hands under each of her breasts and raised them towards me, again with a smile of welcome and invitation. That changed to a snarl as I turned and walked away, pausing only to pick up the telephone. I closed the kitchen door firmly behind me. The knocking on the door began again.

"Who was there?" asked Sheila as soon as I walked back into the darkened living room.

I turned on the lights. "No one you would want to see," I told her.

Sheila looked at the telephone in my hand. "Who you gonna call?" she giggled. "Ghostbusters?"

"I was thinking of the police," I told her seriously.

Sheila was scornful of the idea. "What can you tell them? I've got two dead women banging on my door? They would treat you as a crank, and hang up."

She was probably right, although I rather suspected that Inspector Peake might be less inclined to consider such a call - from me at least - as a hoax. I told her so.

"What is he going to do? Call an armed response unit and shoot them?" Sheila demanded.

I didn't know, and that was obvious from my expression. Sheila began to panic again. "We can't get out!" She started to cry.

I found that more alarming than the constant hammering on the doors, and was goaded into action. "Sheila," I told her firmly: "they can't get in either. I know a man who can help us."

"What is he? Another policeman?"

"No. I'm not really sure what you would call him." A rare flash of humour made me laugh. "Ghostbuster, possibly."

I knew the telephone number by heart and dialled it. The

telephone rang a number of times, before it was answered.

"Yes?" came a cautious voice that I knew quite well from other times like this.

"Hello Eric," I said cheerfully.

There came a deep sigh from the other end of the phone. I had turned on the speaker, and Sheila could hear both sides of the conversation. The sigh did not seem to reassure her at all.

"Mister Jones," Eric said to me. "Would I be surprised to hear that you are in some sort of trouble?"

"Probably not," I replied.

"Does that mean that you are?"

"I have a damsel here in distress who needs rescuing, if you fancy an evening's entertainment," I told him.

Sheila did not look all that impressed at being described as a damsel in distress, but I ignored her expression of disapproval.

"Rescuing? From what? And from where?" asked Eric.

"Well, she's round at my house."

"She needs rescuing from you then, Mister Jones?"

"Hardly, Eric. Actually, I wouldn't mind being rescued at the same time."

Eric's voice lost its heavy note of sarcasm and levity and became more serious at once. "And from what do you both want rescuing?"

"We seem to have some walking dead at the front and back doors."

"And there's - *him*." Sheila added loudly, and somewhat theatrically.

Eric could hear her down the telephone. "Who, or what is this 'him' then?" he asked.

Although I knew Eric could not see me, I shrugged anyway. "No idea," I told him. "But with these two at the doors, to be honest I'm not in a hurry to find out."

"You know that they can't come in, don't you?" Eric asked me.

Sheila stood up then, and seized the telephone from my hand. "It will be nightfall soon, Mister Eric. I don't know what he can do then. Please, if you can help us, just come and help!"

"I don't drive. Do you have a car, miss, as I know that Mister Jones doesn't have one?"

"Yes, yes, I have a car."

"Good! Where is it?" asked Eric.

"It is parked on the road, a few doors down. But it's no use to us."

"Why is that?"

"Because I haven't got the car keys," Sheila said, and started crying again. I passed her a box of tissues.

"Ah. Can you…?" asked Eric.

"No."

"Then I'll have to be inventive," replied Eric cheerfully. "Are you still there, Mister Jones?"

"I'm here, Eric," I told him.

"Knowing you as well as I do, I'm pretty sure that you are going to have half an opened bottle of wine and some mushrooms - possibly a bit past their best? - in the house?"

"Got those."

"Right. Chop the mushrooms finely. Add some chopped or minced onions and a bit of garlic too, and throw in the wine."

"How will cooking help us get out?" demanded Sheila.

"Patience, miss, please," said Eric sternly. "Next, empty all the soil out of a plant pot, and add that. Warm it up on the stove, mix it well, and let it cool. If there's any moss or if you've any vegetables that need throwing away, add them too."

Like Sheila, I was concerned about where this advice was taking us. "Eric, how is this going to help us?"

"You didn't think I was going to tell you to eat it, did you?" Eric started laughing.

Sheila and I didn't see the joke.

"When I arrive at the end of your drive in a taxi, Mister Jones, this is what you will do."

Eric gave his instructions, and we listened carefully. He hung up, and Sheila and I looked at each other.

"The kitchen," I said to her.

"Together," she said firmly.

We walked into the kitchen, and Sheila stopped abruptly at the sight of the naked woman at the back door. As soon as the woman saw me, she again started the lascivious gestures and movements. I tried not to look.

"Do you often get that at your door, Mister Jones?" asked Sheila, a sarcastic edge in her voice. She walked across to the sink and pulled the blind down, so that much of the view was obscured. She also reached across to the back door. The excitement of the woman outside was obvious, but Sheila merely locked the door, and then dropped the key into her pocket. "Just in case you get carried away," she said to me.

I turned away, rather embarrassed, and started finding the ingredients Eric had suggested. When they were simmering in the pan, I looked around the kitchen.

"The only thing missing is some soil," I said.

"You must have a plant somewhere!" said Sheila.

"Actually, I don't. I did have, but it died over winter."

"What did you do with it?"

I brightened up. "I put it in the cellar."

Sheila went pale. "The cellar? You have a cellar here?"

"Well yes, it will be next to yours."

"Mister Jones, whatever you do, do not open that cellar door. In fact, if you have anything that can block the door, let's shove it there now."

"Sheila, it is my cellar. Nothing can get in there."

"Just do it!" she shouted, a little hysterically, I thought.

"Take the pan off the stove," I suggested. "It can cool whilst we block that door."

Sheila dragged the pan of simmering liquid from the cooker, and carried it out into the hall. As she passed the door to my cellar, she suddenly staggered. Faced with the option of catching her or catching the hot pan, I chose the hot pan and managed (at the cost of a couple of minor burns) to stop the contents pouring across the floor of the hall.

"Are you all right, Sheila?" I asked, turning to her. She lay prone on the hall floor, her face chalk white.

"Come for me," she whispered. "Come for me."

I misheard her, and knelt down next to her. I'll comfort you as best I can, Sheila, yes."

She looked at me again, and her eyes were very dark. "He is come for me."

I looked at her, looked at the cellar door, and had pushed a kitchen chair against it in seconds.

She looked up at me, and for a moment was herself again. "Help me, Mister Jones. Help us both! Get me out of here!" She squeezed both her eyes shut. "Quickly! He has crossed into your cellar. Quickly!"

I ran into the living room, and grabbed my keys and wallet. When I came back into the hall, Sheila had risen to her knees and was shaking and panting like a mad thing. I took her arm, and she snapped at me with her teeth, just missing my hand. She shook herself violently like a wet dog would.

Again she opened her eyes, and this time they were her normal bright blue. "Last chance!" she gasped.

I grabbed at the saucepan, and liberally coated us both with the mixture. Then I threw one of her arms around my shoulder for support, grabbed her around the waist and pulled her down the hall, Sheila a dead weight on my arm and shoulder. I dragged open the front door. There stood the cleaner, but she sniffed at us and recoiled for a moment. I pulled the front door closed behind us, and at once Sheila seemed to recover her wits. Run!" she gasped.

I needed no further encouragement. We ran for the garden gate without looking behind to see if her cleaner was following. Miraculously as we ran onto the pavement, a taxi turned into the end of the road. I could see Eric's face, suddenly anxious, peering out of the side window. The taxi stopped, and Eric opened the back door. We ran as fast as we could, Sheila hampered by her lack of fitness and unsuitable shoes, me hampered by my age, and we piled into the back of the taxi. Eric slammed the door and jumped back into the front seat. Sitting up, I could see that Sheila's cleaner was not far behind us, but had now come to a halt.

"Drive!" said Eric, and the taxi driver put his foot on the accelerator. We had escaped.

Chapter Ten

The hospital mortuary was, as ever, a quiet place. The attendant had one of the few jobs in the Health Service where the patients were unlikely to complain, and where there was little fuss or excitement. He had a desk and a small office in the outer room, with the entry to the area where those bodies that had to be stored were kept in chilled cabinets.

The hospital used an internal messenger service for confidential and secure documents rather than entrust some matters to their intranet system, and the messenger was as ever keen to get out of the department after delivering the mail.

"I don't know why you never stop to chat!"

"Look Charlie," replied the messenger, "it's not like you have the best environment is it?"

"It's warm, and I always have coffee going," replied Charlie the mortuary attendant.

"But you don't have any nurses here to chat up. Just a bunch of stiffs. Not the best conversationalists, are they?" said the messenger.

"Well, that might be right. But they don't moan much either!" laughed Charlie.

"Any of them did moan, you'd be right out the door! Anyway, here's tomorrow's list. Oh, and there's an urgent one as well."

The messenger handed over two sheets of paper. Charlie glanced at the first: as the messenger said, it was a list of the bodies that could be released for burial tomorrow, or were wanted for an autopsy. He dropped that sheet onto his desk. The second sheet he examined closely. "It's a bit late today for this, isn't it?" he asked.

The messenger just shrugged. "Don't tell me anything, so they don't. Mind you, wasn't this one that murder victim? Killed by a spear or something, so the rumour goes?"

Charlie looked again at the paper detailing the need for the body to be prepared immediately for an examination a little later that day. "Want to see her?" he asked.

The messenger looked a bit guilty, and out of habit glanced around. "That's..."

"Against regulations, I know," agreed Charlie. "But still, there's only us here."

The messenger had a short internal struggle with himself, and lost. "Go on then. Since you have to anyway."

Charlie looked at the instruction sheet, and verified the name of the body. Then he checked the control list on his computer monitor, and noted the number of the cabinet.

"Come on," he said to the messenger.

Charlie left his desk, and walked to the door separating the front office from the cold area. He tapped the correct security code into the keypad, and opened the door. He allowed the messenger to walk in ahead of him, and closed the door behind them. There was a keypad on the inside of the door as well as the outside, and the messenger looked surprised.

"Don't want any of them getting out and going for a walk, do we?" Charlie said to the messenger.

The latter was clearly beginning to regret his decision to be a voyeur, but it seemed a little late to change his mind. In one corner of the room was a small desk, with a printed list, identifying the cabinets and their occupants. Charlie walked to the desk and checked the list again.

The messenger looked at the wall that was made up of row upon row of small metal doors, each bearing a number.
"Suppose we're all just numbers at some point," he sighed.
"Little boxes, little boxes."

"Yep. Makes you think, sometimes, this job," agreed Charlie.

Beside the desk stood a trolley with adjustable legs. It could be raised or lowered to any of the doors in the blank wall opposite. Charlie pushed the trolley to a door in the second row from the bottom, and using his foot to adjust the height pumped the hydraulic mechanism until the trolley was at the right height.

"Here we go," he said cheerfully. Charlie released the catch securing the cabinet door, and opened it. A thin mist of chilled air spread out, and the messenger shivered.

Charlie reached into the cabinet, and slid the shelf containing the body out onto the trolley. He pushed the trolley slightly away from the cabinet, and closed the door firmly.

"Here we go," he said cheerfully. "Meet Mrs Florence Balsam, late of this parish and recently joined the silent majority."

"I'm not sure that I want to," said the messenger.

Charlie turned to look at him. "That's not very polite, is it? You could be a bit respectful, and say hello to her!" He peered at the messenger, a little surprised. "Here, you don't need to look like that. Haven't you seen one of my customers before? They all look the same after a bit, you know, and there's noting at all to be frightened of. They aint coming to get you, you know!"

The messenger's mouth started working, and he pointed past Charlie's shoulder.

Charlie started laughing.

"Good one, good one!"

The messenger stepped backwards, and Charlie laughed again.

"Let me unzip her for you!" Charlie offered.

"Don't think you need to..." said the messenger.

"Don't be daft," laughed Charlie. He turned back to the trolley, and all of the colour drained from his face.

As he watched in horror, the zip that closed the body bag slowly ran downwards, pulled from the inside of the bag. First one hand, then a second took hold of the fabric, and pulled it away, releasing the body. Slowly, surrounded by the mist caused by the freezing cold of the cabinet evaporating from her naked body, Mrs Balsam sat upright. The messenger wet himself in terror.

"That, that, that..." stammered Charlie.

The messenger was desperately trying to open the door. "What's the code, Charlie?" he shouted.

Mrs Balsam swung her legs down from the trolley, and stood upright on the floor, before turning to face the two men. Charlie backed away.

"The code, Charlie!" shouted the messenger.

Charlie was transfixed. He realised that he could see right through the hole in Mrs Balsam's chest to the desk behind her.

"Help!" shouted the messenger, beating on the door with his hands, and trying to force the lock open.

Charlie could not move. Mrs Balsam had him now in an astonishingly powerful grip.

"Four, four, five" he panted.

The messenger was too busy shouting to hear him. Mrs Balsam dropped Charlie's body at her feet, and stepped over him, her expression entirely blank. The messenger gave up on the door, and stumbled sideways. Mrs Balsam watched him go and try to hide behind the small desk. Then she walked to the door and punched the code that Charlie had revealed with his last breath into the lock. She twisted the handle, and the door opened. Leaving it open, she walked slowly out into the office.

The messenger waited for a minute or two, hardly daring to breathe. Then he dashed for the door, and with a cry of relief passed through it and into the office. The door crashed shut behind him. He stopped, and looked back in terror. No one was there. He made another sound of relief, and turned towards the door to the outside world. Mrs Balsam, no longer appallingly naked but now covered by a white coat from the rack stood waiting for him on the other side of the door to his freedom. She spread her arms wide, and there was nowhere for the messenger to run to. Slowly she advanced on him, and fainting he fell into her final embrace.

*

Ian Evans was carefully filling in a report form in the canteen of the police station when his mobile phone rang. He pulled the phone out of his pocket and studied the caller's number: he gave a muffled curse on realising that it was Inspector Peake, and pressed the green 'accept' button reluctantly.

"Yes, sir?" he said,

"Evans?" demanded Peake.

"Yes, sir?" repeated Evans.

"What did you do with her, Evans?"

"Sir?"

"What did you do with her?"

"Who?"

"That young girl from SOCO."

"Well, I took her to the Balsam house as you told me to, sir. What's wrong?"

"She's not reported back in, and SOCO are blaming me. Guess who I'm blaming?"

Evans sighed. He thought that he could guess.

"Where is she?" demanded Peake.

"I left her at the Balsam's place, sir. Her decision. I brought Miss Balsam back here for you to interview."

"Whatever did you leave her there for?" shouted Peake. "She's got a case load here and everyone is blaming me for her not being on the job!"

"Has no one phoned her, sir?"

"Evans, don't try my patience. Of course she's been phoned. No reply."

Evans looked at his watch. "Sir, it's a long time since I dropped her off there. Surely you've done with Miss Balsam now?"

"And sent her home. But there's no answer from the house line either."

Evans shrugged. "Sir, it's well after six. Probably she's just gone home."

"That Miss Balsam?"

"No, the SOCO girl. Jane something or other."

"Just go and look for her, will you?" ordered Peake. "Get everyone off my back."

"She's probably gone to see some mates, down the pub or gone to get her hair done!" objected Evans. "I'll never find her this evening if she has."

"Well, you left her at the crime scene, so no one can complain at you for that. It was with Sheila's Balsam's permission, wasn't it?"

"Yes, sir. Her express permission, as she had a delivery coming."

"Chairs, it was."

"Sir?"

"We've still got a mighty police presence in the form of Constable Peters sat eating his way into diabetes or a heart attack in a patrol car outside the place."

Evans was confused. "Then why do you want me to go and have a look, sir?"

Peake was suddenly professionally impersonal. "Evans, we know you left a young woman there. She was seen to enter the house and hasn't been seen since and no longer answers her phone. Peters has not observed her leaving the property, and you can recognise her if you... see her. Think about it. But not for long. Just get yourself down there."

Evans suddenly realised that Peake was suggesting that something unpleasant might have happened to the young SOCO officer. If so, he realised, he - Evans - was going to end up feeling responsible. He folded up the report form, and put it in his pocket.

"Yes sir, I'm going now. Have you her home address? I'll check it on the way."

"Right. Wilson will text it to you. Oh, and you can tell Peters to clock off, I've no budget for more time of that sort." Peake hung up.

Evans left the canteen feeling concerned. He had not known the SOCO officer before, but had found her quite attractive on the drive to the Balsam house. By the time he had reached his car in the police station car park, he had received a text with her home address. Smiling slightly to himself, he made sure that he kept the text, rather than delete it. The address was on the side of the town where he lived himself, a fact he noted with some satisfaction. However, it was on the other side of the town to the Balsam house and he had to make a choice: Evans took a coin from his pocket and flipped it. Nodding, he started the car and drove out of the parking space towards the exit.

The rush hour traffic had now eased, the hurrying commuters in the main departed for their homes. Evans was able to pull out into the traffic without difficulty, and headed for the Balsam house. Outside the house, the road contained some cars parked along its length, and Evans was unable to park outside the Balsam house, or indeed outside Mister Jones' residence. He parked some distance away, and had to walk up the road. He stopped outside Mister Jones' house and peered into the older hatchback car parked outside.

"That belongs to the cleaner," said a voice from over his shoulder.

Evans was startled, and banged his head on the window of the car.

"Getting jumpy, Evans? Seen any good spooks recently?" Constable Peters started laughing. Evans reputation had not been improved amongst his colleagues by his involvement in those unusual cases on Inspector Peake's desk.

"Oh yes, very funny," muttered Evans.

"Have you been sent to relieve me then?" asked Peters. "Only my shift is about to end."

"Peake told me to tell you that you can finish here."

"He sent you all the way out here to tell me that?" asked Peters, astonished.

"Nah. Some rubbish about one of the SOCO officers not reporting in. She was here last, so he asked me to check up."

"Oh, that thin girl who came with you earlier? I told him on the phone that I thought she was still there."

Evans looked at Peters. "Well why didn't he tell you to go and knock on the door?"

"He did. I got no reply. I tried asking the cleaner when she came out but she couldn't express herself coherently. And that Miss Balsam and your mate Jones ran off before I could talk to them."

Evans looked puzzled.

"Anyway," carried on Peters, "it's not my problem. See you around." Peters walked back to his marked patrol car, started the engine and drove off leaving Evans looking thoughtfully at the Balsam house.

"Well, best I get it done and then I can go home," Evans

muttered to himself.

He opened the gate at the end of the drive, and leaving it open walked down the short drive to the front door. To his surprise, there was a click and it opened slightly as he approached.

"Hello?" Evans called.

He pushed gently on the door and it opened a little more. Inside the house, the hallway was full of early evening shadows, and he could see little.

"Jane?" he shouted.

There was no reply.

"Jane? It's Ian Evans."

The shadows seemed to thicken and become darker, but Evans dismissed that as a product of his imagination.

"Police!" he shouted. "Is anyone home?"

The door opened a little more, and Evans gave the bottom of the door a gentle push with his boot. The door opened fully, and Evans drew his baton: the door had swung back fully against the wall and he didn't think anyone could have been standing behind it. So how had the door moved? Evans stepped inside the hall and checked behind the door. As he suspected, there was no one there.

"Police!" he shouted again, and stepped cautiously down the hall.

The front door suddenly slammed shut behind him, and Evans jumped at the sound. He turned to look at the door, but there was still no one else in the hall. He swallowed and took a fresh grip on his police baton, raising it slightly. Looking around the dark hall, he could dimly see a light switch on the wall. He reached out and pressed it but nothing happened, no illumination cleared the darkness before him.

At the end of the hall, beyond the stairs, there were two doors: both were closed. Evans walked down the dark hall with a steady stride. The first door he came to opened on the left. Evans reached out with his left hand, and turned the door handle. Then using his baton, he slowly opened the door and looked inside.

The living room was empty. Evans looked around carefully. Over one chair he could see a coat that he recognised as Jane's. A handbag lay beside it, and he thought that looked familiar too. Was that the bag she had held in his car earlier? He thought furiously, but could not be certain. He began to wonder if Inspector Peake was right, and something was amiss. The silence of the house was unnerving, and the shifting shadows seemed to conceal secrets. He shivered.

Evans left the living room. Now walking softly, he crossed the hall and put his left hand on the door handle of the kitchen door. Was that his imagination, or was there a soft sound from the other side of the door? The hairs on the back of his neck rose, and he shivered again. Once more using his baton, he pushed the door open. The evening sun was shining through the kitchen window, and so the kitchen was better lit than either the hall or the living room.

Evans looked around the kitchen, but it was immediately clear that no one was there either. "I'm sure that I heard something," he muttered aloud, feeling comforted by the small sound of his own voice.

He looked around the kitchen again, and the door of a tall cupboard to his left moved slightly. The door catch clicked. "That's what I heard," he said, again aloud to himself. Evans reached out with his baton, and touched the door. He was about to push it shut, when he wondered if he should open the door instead? But then he froze. Upstairs, from the room directly above, he had heard an unmistakeable footfall. Evans left the kitchen, and stood at the bottom of the stairs. "Police!" he shouted. "Is anyone up there?"

When there was no reply, he slowly set off up the stairs. When he reached the top, he looked around carefully. The landing ran along a wall to the front of the house, and three doors opened off it. He had been in Mister Jones' home before, a number of times, and rightly assumed that this adjoining house would have exactly the same design. The nearest door would be the front bedroom. Carefully he opened the door, and stepped inside. He was struck with astonishment at the sight of the room. The wall directly opposite him, the wall adjoining Mister Jones' home, looked as if it had received a frenzied attack. Long strips of the flowered wallpaper hung in shreds in those places where the paper had not simply been ripped from the wall completely. Deep gouges had been made in the plaster, and in the very center of the wall was a large hole. Even from the doorway, Evans could see through the hole, but also see that an attempt to block it up had been made in the corresponding room in the other house.

Plaster and dust lay scattered all across the bed, along with shreds of the wallpaper. Ian Evans could not begin to think how the damage had been done: but clearly it was not very recent. No dust hung in the air, the clothes that lay on the bed and on the chair were covered in the debris, and had not been disturbed. The room faced the front of the house, and the evening shadows fell across the bed. As Evans stared around the room, the shadows on the wall beside him - and out of his vision - grew darker, denser, and started to coalesce. Slowly the shadows began to rise up the wall.

Evans drew a deep, uneven breath and stepped backwards out of the room. He pulled the door closed in front of him, and then steadied himself. He knew that he had been looking on the bed and the wall for one thing - the sight of spilt blood. He was only slightly reassured that he had seen none. The next door lay a few steps along the landing, and he correctly surmised that this would be the door to the rear bedroom.

Once more, he released the latch with his left hand and opened the door slowly and carefully with his baton. As the door opened he could see the bed. It was immaculately made, with one corner of the duvet turned down. The door opened a little more. It was clear that this room had not been molested in the same manner as the other, for it seemed to be pristine. Looking back at the bed as he pushed harder on the door, he could see a shadow cast across the bed, a human shadow. He knew the rear window caught the late sun, as did the kitchen: this was a shadow cast by someone standing at the window.

"Hello?" he asked, with only a hint of a tremor in his voice. "Police. Are you all right?"

There was no reply, and the shadow on the bed was motionless. Evans pushed the door all the way open and stepped into the room. The evening sun through the bedroom window was strong and he squinted at the person standing at the window.

"Why, it's Ian Evans, come all this way to see me."

The figure stepped away from the window, and released from the glare Evans immediately recognised Jane's face. He also realised with a shock that she was completely naked.

"Why, It's Ian Evans," said Jane again.

Despite his shock, Evans noticed that her voice sounded quite different. Whilst recognisably her own, her tone carried a heavy sensuality he had not heard from her earlier that day.

"Have you come all this way to look for me?" asked Jane, taking another step towards him.

"Inspector Peake..." started Evans. He realised that his voice sounded strained, cleared his throat and tried to take control over his vocal chords. "Inspector Peake said that you had not checked in and that you were not answering your mobile phone."

Jane ran her hands slowly up and down her sides and her legs. "I don't seem to have it on me," she said.

Evans nodded. He could see that.

"Why don't you ring him for me now?" she asked. "You can tell him that there is nothing he needs worry about."

"Isn't there something he should worry about?" asked Evans.

"Oh no, there's nothing at all to worry about. Quite the opposite."

Evans pulled his mobile phone from his pocket, and pressed the redial button.

"Evans? Evans? That you is it?" Inspector Peake's voice sounded thin and far away through the speaker of the phone.

"Yes, sir. I'm just with Jane now."

"Is she all right?" demanded Peake.

Jane walked towards Ian Evans, swaying her hips.

"Oh yes, she's fine, sir," replied Evans, unable to take his eyes from the girl.

"Right. I'll tell SOCO and then she's their problem." Peake disconnected the call.

"Do I look like a problem?" purred Jane, as Evans fumbled with the telephone, trying to replace it in his pocket. "Or do I look like an opportunity?"

"Jane..." Evans took a step backwards. He reached out for the door, and discovered to his surprise that it had somehow closed behind him. Jane was very close to him now, and he could smell her entrancing perfume. He could not resist the urge to look down at the curves and shadows of her body, and she smiled in wicked delight.

"Jane, I don't know you... well enough for..." he stammered.

"What does that matter? Here we are, the two of us, what does ought else matter?"

Evans somehow noted the archaic word in her sentence, but it didn't register fully.

Jane again ran her hands up and down and around her body, and Evans' breathing quickened, and he fought against the rising tide of lust that threatened to overwhelm him.

"It is instinct, isn't it, Ian? Your instincts tell you what you should do now, don't they?" Her hands reached for him, and unbuckled his dark jacket. "I can see that they do. Instinct is all that matters now, is it not?" She slid his jacket from his shoulders, and reached for his belt. "Our ancient appetites draw us, lead us on, lead us in... surrender to those instincts Ian, become one with them..."

She unbuckled his belt and undid the button on the top of his trousers. Evans' breathing became ragged and uneven, and Jane released his clothing... she took both of his hands in hers, and he jerked. A shock like a lightning bolt coursed through him at her touch. Jane tightened her grip on his hands, and pulled him closer towards her as she stepped backwards towards the bed. The lust pouring into him through her hands met his own inner demon and exploded with power, rocked through his mind and suppressed all his inhibitions and better nature, consuming him.

"It is a celebration, a worship, Ian. Come, worship with me. Worship the god Vulang with me."

Ian Evans did not resist as she pulled him down onto the bed, not even when he looked into her eyes and saw that they were now crimson, with black pupils.

Chapter Eleven

Eric relaxed against the front seat of the taxi, and smiled widely. The driver stared at him with suspicion.

"Now what?" demanded the taxi driver.

"Could you take us all back to my place, where you picked me up, please? " asked Eric.

"It all seems a bit odd, this," grumbled the driver. Through his rear view mirror he could see Maria standing in the road, watching the taxi drive away.

"Why?" asked Eric, innocently. "You picked me up, we picked up some friends of mine, now we go back to my place."

"It looked like they were running away from someone, to me. And they smell something awful!"

"I'm quite sure that these two have done nothing to be ashamed about," Eric said reassuringly.

I looked at Sheila, who was far from relaxed beside me. "Nothing at all," I agreed.

"You see?" said Eric brightly. He smiled at us both again, and then turned to look with apparent interest out of the front window of the taxi.

The rest of the fairly short journey to Eric's home was spent in silence. Eric paid the taxi driver, and added a large enough tip to satisfy the driver. I opened the rear door of the car, and helped

Sheila to get out. The driver lost no time in driving away and leaving us on the pavement.

I looked at Sheila, and saw that she was staring with interest at Eric. I remembered that, whilst he and I had met several times, she had not seen him before. As was his wont, he was dressed in a cream linen suit with a plain shirt, and looked cool and unflustered. We, however, were neither and he recognised that swiftly. With his usual courtesy, Eric opened the gate to his front garden and ushered us inside. He led the way down to the path to his front door, and unlocked it. He pushed the door open with his left hand, and turned to Sheila.

"Please, enter and be welcome - and safe here."

Sheila looked at me, a transparent question in her face.

"Sheila, trust me on this:" I said to her. "Eric's house is as safe as anywhere we are going to find."

That seemed to be enough for her, and she tried to step into the hall. Eric's eyes grew wide and he looked at her with some alarm as she struggled to step past the frame of his door, over his threshold. I reached out to her, but Eric suddenly knocked my hand aside.

"Don't touch her. Mister Jones," he said quietly.

We both watched Sheila struggle to take a step forward. Finally, as if stepping through treacle, she managed to move forward and she finally walked across the threshold into the light, cool hall with some relief. The atmosphere of the house affected her immediately: I could see the tension in her evaporate like a mist, and her body relaxed. I actually feared that she might fall, and started forward to reach out for her, but Eric threw his arm out and stopped me again.

"Down the hall and take the first door on the right please, miss," Eric said to her.

Sheila walked slowly down the hall. Eric drew me to one side and without speaking, pointed to the floor. At the front door to his house, a dark shadow moved, and with some shock I realised that it was Sheila's shadow: now parted from her as she walked into Eric's home. I looked at him and silently, grimly, he nodded to me. We watched the shadow writhe on the floor, and I stepped back in case it touched me. Eric raised one foot and deliberately stamped on the shadow. It flowed up around and all over his shoe as if to overwhelm his foot but then froze as if pinned to the floor; then it slowly faded and vanished. Eric waved a hand at me, and that was my invitation to enter his home. I stepped across his threshold and I paused only to slip my shoes from my feet before walking down his hall. Eric nodded at me in appreciation of my good manners, as he himself changed his outdoor shoes for some sandals. I looked at him quizzically, and he smiled and held up one shoe. I saw that the heel had a strip of bright silver inlaid around the heel and the side of the shoe in one continuous band. Sheila looked back when she saw we had not immediately followed her.

"Oh, I'm sorry," she said to Eric. "I'll take these off right away." She lifted one foot awkwardly, and fumbled at the strap on the back of the shoe.

Eric smiled, and waved her apology away. "Go into the living room, and sit down by the fire, miss."

"Sheila. My name is Sheila."

"Sheila, then." Eric gave a small, courteous bow, then closed his front door. He waved one hand over the back of the door in a pattern that was clearly familiar to him and muttered something I could not hear.

"My defences stand well, Mister Jones," Eric said softly to me, so that he was not overheard. "What came here with her could not enter here. And I made sure that it could not linger to wait for her to leave."

"What came here with her?" I asked, confused.

Eric gave me a stern look. "How well do you know this lady, Mister Jones? Are you involved with her in any way?"

"Eric!" I was slightly shocked. "She is much, much younger than I am, so no, I am not 'involved' with her. She is my next door neighbour."

Eric seemed to be rather relieved by that. "I just wanted to know if you were romantically involved with this girl, that is all."

"Why? Is she in danger?"

"Oh yes. A very great deal of danger. And in turn she could become dangerous to those around her. Mister Jones. Meaning you."

I looked at him open mouthed, but he just smiled enigmatically and walked down the hall, leaving me beside his front door. Eric walked to the door of his living room, and I caught up with him in time to hear him start talking to Sheila.

"Good afternoon, or perhaps it is evening now? We haven't been introduced. Mister Jones was remiss in his good manners for once, wasn't he? My name is Eric."

"Hello Eric. I'm Sheila, Sheila Balsam."

"I am very pleased to meet you, Sheila, and I think that Mister Jones did exactly the right thing in bringing you here to me today."

Sheila looked at him in surprise and with suspicion. "What has he told you about me?" she asked.

"Why, nothing more than you needed help. And I am quite sure that he was right, now that I have met you."

Eric turned and looked at me as I stood in the doorway. He beckoned to me to come closer, into the room. I had been in that room several times and had always felt a wonderful sense of peace and security. Sheila stood beside the fireplace, not yet having accepted Eric's invitation to be seated. Even in the summer a small fire burned brightly in the gate and somehow the sight gave me comfort and reassurance.

"Please," he waved to me to join them before the fireplace. I did so.

Eric looked directly at Sheila. "Would you please kneel before the fire with us?"

I caught the 'us' in that sentence and gently went down on both knees before the fire and sat back on my heels. Eric did the same and a moment later, looking slightly bemused, Sheila followed us. Eric reached to his right, and picked up a basket containing several small pieces of wood.

"Please take one piece and add it to the fire," he told Sheila, offering her the basket.

She looked at the basket, and then at Eric, clearly wondering if this was a practical joke or if I had brought her to the home of a madman.

"You first, Sheila," I said gently.

Finally she smiled as if to humour us and did as she was asked. The flames licked around the small piece of wood as she placed it in the grate and she quickly withdrew her hand. Shortly afterwards a pleasant aromatic scent arose, and she breathed in deeply. I too took a small piece of wood from the basket and added it to the fire. Eric did the same, and returned the basket to its place just out of sight. He motioned us to stand up, and we did so. Next Eric moved slightly so that he could reach behind the chair to his right. A small table was there, and from the table he took a large bunch of dried herbs. He pushed the end of the bunch into the flames, and as the herbs lit quickly withdrew them and waved them around in a circle. The flames were replaced by rising smoke scented with sage and lavender. Eric waved the bunch of herbs up and down Sheila, both front and back. She seemed to stifle her amusement but her eyes carried on laughing as Eric repeated the procedure with me and then finally did the same to himself.

"Please, be seated now," said Eric.

Sheila dropped into one chair, and looked at him. He looked back, and then burst out laughing. Surprised, she could no longer contain her laughter, and joined him. Eric sat in the other chair, the first time I had ever known him be less than a perfect host. I looked around the room. A stool was placed against one wall, and I stepped across and picked it up. I turned back to the fire, now crackling merrily and spreading a pleasant and clean applewood scent into the room, and joined the other two before the fire.

"Mister Jones, I am sorry, wherever are my manners?" asked Eric.

I waved away his apology.

"Sheila - I may call you Sheila?" Eric continued. "I can understand why you think my little ritual here is amusing. Let's just say that it has a point, and then forget about it, all right?"

Sheila nodded.

"Now, my friend Mister Jones here called me and said that you were in some distress, is that right?"

Sheila's amusement faded. "Yes, yes it is, Eric."

"Now, I know Mister Jones, and he tends to get distressed only by fairly specific things. And if he says that he needs rescuing, it usually means that he does. Your friend - and mine - Mister Jones has bumped into things that, well, 'go bump in the night' before: he knows how to recognise these things and he knows that I can help in these times."

"Why?" demanded Sheila.

"Why? Because that is what I do", replied Eric simply and convincingly. "Now, why don't you tell me your story? From the beginning, right up to the time you joined me in the taxi, running away from something."

I had always known Eric to be terribly careful with his choice of words, and his use of 'something' rather than 'someone' I marked down for future reference.

Sheila laughed. "It will seem, well, rather silly now." She looked around the room, her glance lingering on the woven hanging of Vishnu fixed to the wall opposite the fireplace. "This is all so, well normal."

Eric clasped his hands together, and leant towards her, sincerity radiating from him. "Sheila, this seems normal to you now, you are able to laugh and relax, because of what you left behind at my door."

She looked at him, perplexed. "I don't understand." But even I, unused to women as I am, could find a hint of evasion in her voice and in the way her eyes refused to meet his.

"Yes, you do," said Eric simply. "I know what you left at my door, Sheila Balsam. I know what you brought here: and I know that Mister Jones was right to bring you here: because what you carried with you could not enter this house, and when you did - of your own free will - you became free of it."

Sheila's mouth dropped open and she just stared at Eric. He stood, and walked around his chair to the small table that lay there. The table held a silver tray, a number of tall glasses as some bottles of spring water. I remembered from previous visits that the water would be cool and refreshing, with a hint of flavour. Suddenly I felt very thirsty indeed, and when Eric brought the tray around his chair with the glasses filled with the water, I could tell that Sheila felt the same.

Eric offered the tray first to Sheila, who took a glass. She first

209

sipped the water, then downed the whole glass in one and suddenly looked embarrassed. Eric whipped the tray away from me before I could take a glass, and offered it again to Sheila. She put the empty glass on the tray, and when he did not remove it, took a second glass. Eric let me take the remaining glass of water, and going back to the table filled another for himself. He sat down, and sipped at his glass.

"Now," he said to Sheila, "please, from the start of the tale."

"But if you know...?"

"I know what came with you. Not the story of how it came to be there."

Sheila seemed embarrassed and afraid at the same time.

"Do not worry," Eric told her. "What you brought is gone. It is not waiting for you when you go out of the front door."

I was still very confused by all this, and said so.

"You see, Sheila?" said Eric gently. "Your neighbour, and the one who saved you by bringing you to me, would like to know what happened."

"Oh well," Sheila said. "It will all come out in the end, so I might as well get on with it." She sipped from her glass, thinking.

"But you must promise to tell me the whole story. All of it."

"I promise," agreed Sheila, and began. "Three, no four days ago now, I was in a shop not too far from here. A touristy, arty, boutique I thought it was. My attention had been caught by an old fashioned painting in the window, which was not for sale, and I went in. Inside I found some terracotta statuettes. One was of a unicorn, and I was immediately drawn to it."

I had been watching Sheila, but my attention was caught by Eric's reaction. It seemed to be one of recognition, which I found very surprising. Sheila continued.

"Although the statuettes seemed very, very, old I was assured that they were all genuinely for sale, and not looted or stolen or anything. I don't know what it was about that statuette of the unicorn, but I felt that I must buy it. And I did, although I could not really afford it and I knew that my mother would kick up the most awful fuss about it."

I was going to quietly tell Eric about Sheila's mother, but he waved me to silence.

"Then it was delivered. But the strange thing was that the paperwork, especially the invoice, wasn't there. I opened all the packaging myself to look, but it wasn't there. Perhaps it would come in the post I decided and forgot about it. Anyway, mother did indeed kick up the most awful fuss, and we had a terrible row about it."

"What did she want?" asked Eric, gently.

"She wanted the unicorn to be sent back. We could not afford it, and she didn't like it. But I did." Sheila clasped her hands together. "Mr Eric, you must understand something. I - we - I am not very well off. My job doesn't pay very well, and my mother's pensions paid most of the bills. I insisted on contributing, and that meant that I didn't have much money. Well, any money, really. So I didn't buy things for myself, because I couldn't. Then I saw this, and I wanted something for myself so much..." she broke off and started to cry. From nowhere, Eric produced a box of tissues and she took it with a grateful look.

"I'm sorry," she said.

Eric reached out and took one of her hands in both of his. "Sheila, don't apologise for your grief."

"It isn't my grief, Mr Eric. That was not grief for my mother, just fear for what will happen now to me, and knowing that it is all my own fault for giving in to wanting something so much. I won't be able to pay the bills, I will have to leave my home, and all because I was foolish and wanted something that I couldn't afford and didn't need as a treat."

I wanted to say something, but that would perhaps have been foolish too, and Eric motioned me to silence with an urgent gesture.

"What happened next?" Eric asked.

Sheila was more matter of fact now that she had expressed what worried her most. "Next, my mother died."

If she had expected Eric to be shocked, she was disappointed. "How?" he asked, without inflexion in his voice. I knew him of old, and knew that when he spoke in that apparently disinterested, neutral tone he was passionately interested in the reply.

"She was stabbed, or maybe run through with some sort of weapon. Perhaps a spear? Something sharp anyway. I found her in the kitchen the following morning, and at once I called Mister

Jones here to help me."

I opened my mouth to add something at this point and again Eric waved me to silence, this time with a hint of impatience. He motioned Sheila to continue.

"Mister Jones called the police, and they came and took her away. They asked me a lot of questions, none of which I could really answer. I had heard my mother go downstairs in the night, but otherwise I was asleep all night."

Sheila sipped more water. "Anyway, that evening - last night, although it seems so long ago now, I could not face sleeping in the house alone. So I begged Mister Jones to stay at his house instead, and he kindly let me have his spare room. During the night, there was a storm, and I had quite a bad night. Then I had the most awful dream."

"Dream?" asked Eric.

"Dream," Sheila said firmly.

"Tell me about it?" asked Eric gently.

"Nothing much to tell, really. In it I, well, I met this man. He was lovely, and he told me he was divine. Obviously I didn't pay much attention to that, and it was just a dream."

"Indeed."

"The next morning I woke up, and there had been some storm damage to the houses. I went home to check on mine, and the police wanted to talk to me again."

"Quite understandable," commented Eric.

Now Sheila seemed to be entering a part of the story she felt less comfortable telling. "This is like a dream, too. In fact, I am not entirely sure that it was not a dream, and that I didn't over react." She again sipped at her water. "When I came home after seeing the police again, one of the police officers was in my house, in fact she was in the cellar. And she… she… any way, I ran. The only place that I could think of to run to was Mister Jones' house next door. I don't know how, but the man from my dream was following me and I didn't know how to escape. But Mister Jones rang you, and you came for us in a taxi. And now here we are." Sheila brightened up considerably at the end of her tale, but Eric appeared to be downcast.

"Miss Balsam, I do not think I can help you further," he said.

"Eric!" I objected, but he waved me to silence, this time with an annoyed expression. Sheila remained seated, but silent.

"I asked you, and you agreed, to tell me everything. I know that you did not."

"I did," Sheila replied, but in a small and unconvincing tone.

"You did not. You did not tell me about the cellar in your house. You did not tell me about whatever it was that was chasing you to the taxi, and you did not tell me about what alarmed Mister Jones - who is not easily alarmed like that, I can assure you - and made him call me for help. I can only help if you tell me everything. And you will be surprised how much I might already know."

Sheila looked at Eric in alarm. "Are you a mind reader?" she asked.

214

"No, Miss Balsam. I am one who has spent a lot of time with the occult though, and one who has spent a lot of time dealing with the consequences for those who unwittingly get drawn into things best left alone. You are one of those. As are others. Your silence now endangers them. Will you not talk?"

Sheila coughed to cover her confusion. Eric leaned back in his chair and looked implacable.

"Is it safe?" asked Sheila, still in that quiet and tremulous tone.

"Yes!" replied Eric forcefully. "Entirely safe. Nothing ever enters this house without my express permission. Nothing!"

"He said his name was..."

"I know his name."

Sheila looked up at Eric, her eyes wide. "How?"

"Later."

"He wanted..."

"I know what he wanted, Miss Balsam. Did he get it?"

"No."

Eric smiled then, and looked very satisfied. "Very good!"

"Not from me," continued Sheila. "But he did from Maria, and from the police woman."

Eric frowned. "Maria?"

"Maria was the lady sent round by the cleaning agency to clean up after the police had put that powder stuff everywhere. I don't know when or how, but he killed her too. At least I think he did. She seemed quite dead when I pushed her body down into the cellar, and drew a chalk circle around it, as he told me to."

"Ah." Now Eric seemed satisfied.

"Was Maria the woman who was banging on my front door, and who then chased us up the path to the taxi?" I asked. This time Eric did not object to my interruption.

"Yes," agreed Sheila.

"But you said you thought she was dead!" I objected.

"So I did. I believe she is dead."

"And what about the naked woman at my back door?" I asked. "Who was she?"

"That was the policewoman, I think," Sheila told me.

"And in my cellar?" I asked.

"That would have been him." She turned to Eric: "That is everything. Truly."

Eric smiled at her. "Not quite, but it is enough. Now I know enough."

"Well I don't," I told him. "Can you enlighten me?"

"Of course! But you might need a few more incarnations first, Mister Jones!"

"Very funny, Eric. What is going on, and who is this 'he' you both talk about?"

"The word 'he' is probably not really accurate, Mister Jones: but it will do for now, at this time. His name is Vulang."

I notice Sheila shake a little at the name, and I am sure that Eric noticed that too.

"He is a demon, one of the fallen ones. Or maybe just an entity so old that it is hard to tell the difference. But demon is a good word, for Vulang has but one purpose, one desire, one goal."

"What is that?" asked Sheila.

"To release the demon that lies within each of us. We all have, deep inside for the most part, something we suppress. It is the basest part of our natures, often our worst side, and Vulang delights in calling to that within us, to unchain it and let it free to rule us. For each it is a different thing, but Vulang has the power to see that within each of us and to let us set it free - so that we become slaves to our worst instincts."

"How do you know all of this?" asked Sheila. "And how did this Vulang come to live inside my unicorn?"

Eric looked her straight in the face, examining her eyes. "I know this because I have met and fought him before. I am the one who Bound him within that unicorn statuette and buried him under the desert. How he came to be offered for sale, I do not know. But it is Fate that drives us together again."

Eric stood, and walked away from the fire to face the portrait of Vishnu. "Vulang, freed could make this a terrible place. Lust, greed envy, hatred and violence: these things he loves and they feed him and make him grow stronger. First though, to escape from the prison I made for him he would need a lot of power. Power he can only get by taking blood."

Sheila's hand flew to her mouth, and Eric turned towards her. "He has started drinking, hasn't he?"

Sheila nodded. "Maria, for certain. The police woman, and probably my mother too."

"He can take blood through force, but without a lot of it he will not be able to beak free of my Binding, or at least not for long. I must stop him before he can break the enchantment," Eric said in a grim tone.

"How can we do that?" I asked.

Eric nodded at me in appreciation of my offer to help. "I will tell you," he said.

Chapter Twelve

Ian Evans opened his eyes. He yawned, and stretched in the dark room, and for a moment wondered where he was. Jane's warm body left him in no doubt, and the memories flooded back. He sat up, and immediately her arms enfolded him and pulled him back down onto the bed. The bedroom door was slightly open, a dim light entered the room casting a glow across the bed, and in that light he could see her face

"Not yet, lover," she murmured into his ear.

"Jane, we're in someone else's house!" he objected.

"So? She's not here."

"How do you know?"

"I would know," she purred.

He looked at her face as she climbed on top of him, but her eyes were dark as jet. Ian puzzled over a memory of her face, he was sure that her eyes had been glowing, a crimson colour before he ceased to pay attention to them. "Your eyes..." he said aloud.

"You don't like them?"

"It's just the colour they are now isn't what I recall."

"Don't be silly Ian. Anyway, there's something much more important to think about."

"Like?"

Jane swung one bare leg over Ian's body, and sat on top of him. She stared down at him, her strange dark eyes unnerving him. "Give yourself over to absolute pleasure, Ian. It's the most important thing. It is the only thing, I've come to realise."

"Jane..."

"We live such little lives, Ian. They don't last long, do they, and then back we go to the dust that spawned us. What else is there to do but to enjoy our time?"

Jane wriggled her hips whilst she sat on him, and Ian did indeed enjoy the sensation.

"Everything else is a distraction, Ian. Whatever else there is in your life but pleasure, cast it aside, let it go. It matters not, and interferes with the pure sensations you should experience whilst you can."

Ian reached up, and grasped her firm body. She gasped with pleasure, although he recognised that it was a false sound for his benefit, to extend her argument, to sway him.

"I don't think that way, Jane," he said seriously. "That's why I became a Police Officer. There *are* other things than lust, than fun, than frivolity."

"And these things matter to you? Whatever are they, these ideas? Tell them to me Ian, and I will show you how they are frail ideas to be set aside."

"Duty. Compassion for others, helping, sharing..." gasped Ian.

On the wall behind him, unseen, shadows started to run

together, coalesce, and climb up the wall. Jane looked at them, and a crimson glow began to outline her eyes.

"Children are innocent, free of such distractions, Ian. They live so naturally, so free. They only think of what is fun for them to do, and of their play. We should be like them, for we, even grown as we are, we are but as children inside the universe. Like them we should play without fear, without responsibility, naturally." She stared down at him with an intensity Ian found hard to match. Against his will, he found his resolution crumbling, as her body drew a response from his own.

"You see?" she purred. "Your body agrees with me. Join with me."

"Jane..."

"Lust is the driving force behind our lives. Live it with me now!" She flung back her head and laughed.

Again Ian felt a pressure inside his head, but this time he fought back and resisted.

"I don't think that way, Jane. I won't think that way."

The crimson glow faded from Jane's eyes, which became entirely black again.

"Very well. I haven't convinced you." Jane lowered her body down until her face was only inches from his, and her jet eyes stared into Evans' with a frightening intensity. "But I know a man who can. More than a man, a god. To him you will yield, Ian."

Jane rolled off Ian, off the bed, and onto the floor where she writhed for a moment and then stood upright. A dressing gown lay on the end of the bed, and she pulled it around herself, somewhat to Evans' disappointment. She noted his reaction, and she gave him a triumphant look.

"The great god Vulang will enter you Ian, and fill you with his glorious spirit, as he did for me. You will be free then, your innermost hidden dreams will be yours to make real."

She flung up her arms in celebration. Behind the bed, the shadows formed the image of a tall man, with a horn growing from his brow, and the shadowman stepped away from the wall, and stared down at Evans with an impassive gaze. Evans followed Jane's stare, and saw the shadowman looming over him. As the horn dipped towards him, Evans reacted. He rolled sharply away from the threat, and fell off the bed on the opposite side as the horn struck down, narrowly missing his left arm.

Panting with sudden fear, Evans threw himself at the bedroom door, and wrenched it open, hoping for escape. But there stood the silent figures of Maria and Mrs Balsam, their eyes a deep crimson in the presence of their Master. He stopped in shock. How long had they been there? He had heard no sound from the landing earlier. They reached out for him, and seized his arms. Jane came to stand beside him, his own handcuffs in her hands. Maria and Mrs Balsam spun Evans around, holding his arms firmly. Jane quickly slapped the handcuffs around his wrists. Behind her the shadowman loomed imperiously, tall and threatening. Evans heard no instruction, but the three women clearly heard his order. Maria grabbed Evans by the wrist, and pulled irresistibly. Evans had no choice but to follow.

First Mrs Balsam, then Maria, next Evans and finally Jane: the procession stepped slowly but inexorably along the landing and down the stairs. Evans stumbled in the semi darkness, but his three captors had no such trouble. The door to the kitchen was open, and Mrs Balsam walked through. Once inside the kitchen she opened the door to the cellar, and pulled the cord that turned on the dim bulb. She vanished into the cellar, and descended the steps, whilst the other waited in the kitchen. Evans pulled hard at Maria, but her grip was unnaturally powerful and he found himself unable even to shake her arm.

"Ian, Ian, stop it," Jane chided him. "You will only hurt yourself. Maria will not harm you. None of us will harm you. Why should we?"

"What are you doing with me?" demanded Ian. He looked at the open door into the cellar with fear. He had no wish to go through that door, as he felt strongly that he might not come out again.

"You are going to join us, Ian, that's all. The great god will fill you with his spirit, as he did with us, and you will be free of these tiresome ideas, free to be whoever you really are. Think of it, Ian: we say that freedom is the thing we all desire most, yet we bind ourselves around with petty rules, imagined boundaries, and say that freedom resides there. It doesn't."

Jane flung out her arms and turned her face upwards. "Freedom is out there to be taken, to be loved, to be lived. Freedom is doing whatever you most want to do at any time, anywhere, just because. The great god will strike these fetters from your mind, Ian, and release you to be free. To be yourself, without inhibition, without constraint. Think of it! Think how joyous your life will be, when you can follow every impulse, wherever it leads you!"

Maria pulled Ian forward to the top of the steps, and he stared down into the cellar for the first time. Mrs Balsam was walking slowly around the glowing golden circle, lighting the tall black candles in between each of the ornately carved chairs.

Ian started to fight, but even though he was a strong young man, and physically fit, he was unable to make an impression on his captor. She started down the stone steps, and he had no choice but to follow her, stumbling as he went. Her crimson eyes granted her the vision Evans lacked and Maria made no allowance for the dim light. Stumbling, Evans lost his balance. He fell hard onto Maria's back, and she finally lost her footing. They tumbled painfully down the last of the steps, and Maria lost her grip on Evans' arm.

Evans scrambled to his feet, and barged Jane to one side as she came down the last few steps. Having his hands cuffed did not help his balance, but he recovered and ran as fast as he could back up the steps towards the door. Gasping for breath, he threw himself at the door, but although it shook, it did not open. Evans looked wildly back to the cellar. The candles were now all lit, and Mrs Balsam and Jane had both taken their places in the wooden chairs. The Master Chair or Throne was now also occupied, and as Ian watched the shadowman grew in size, and definition: his horn was darkness itself, even against the darkness within the cellar.

With a sob of fear, Evans threw himself again against the unyielding door before falling to the floor. He could hear Maria climbing the back up the stairs to reach him. Desperately he bunched his legs and kicked out as hard as he could. Finally the door cracked open, but on hitting the door so hard, Evans had slid backwards across the small landing. Unable to use his hands for balance or to save himself, he realised that he was about to fall over the edge of the landing and drop the distance down to the stone floor below. He welcomed the idea as a last means of escape. As he started to fall, Maria's unnaturally strong hands grabbed his thigh and stopped him.

Evans didn't know if he should be grateful or not as Maria took hold of him and pulled him back onto the landing, then forced him to stand up. He shook his head violently in rejection, but she forced him down the stone steps ahead of her. He stumbled: she roughly shook his shoulder and kept him upright, keeping a tight grip on his upper arm. At the bottom of the steps she swung him around and almost threw him into the centre of the circle, ensuring that he had no chance to scuff or mark the circle as he passed. Evans fell full length on the floor, and as he did so the shadowman left his throne and stood upright. He touched the circle with one foot, and at once the entire ring began to glow with a strong golden light. Dimly, through the light, Evans saw Maria walk around the circle and sit in one of the remaining two chairs.

The shadowman raised both his arms, and the women stood. Through the light Evans realised that the shadowbody was now fearsomely real.

"Hail to the great god Vulang!" chorused all three women loudly. It was the first time Evans had heard the other two women speak, and he was amazed at their voices. They sounded harsh as ravens, yet full of power and he realised in horror, also full of hatred and the love of causing pain. Fear overwhelmed him.

*

Eric poured more lemon flavoured water for both Sheila and me. He resumed his seat and stared into the heart of the small fire. "I remember when I bound the demon that first time," he said reflectively.

"Eric," I said quietly, "you said that was in a previous life."

"As I did, as it was, Mister Jones."

I could not think of anything to say to that, so I remained silent.

"It was in a desert, a hot desert. I had prepared myself for the confrontation. I had researched the power of this demon, and summoned what strength I possessed. The things that I wanted I had collected and I had purified for my use. But this demon was strong, stronger than I had thought. That, I fear, is the cause of our present difficulty. I contained the power of the demon, and I performed the Binding. But the demon made it so hard that I could not take my time. I created my circle of power, but Vulang resisted and nearly broke my circle. Such a thing had not happened before, not to me. So I fear that I left a weakness in the Bind. That weakness was blood, of course. If Vulang could start to take blood, he could leave the statuette to which I bound him for a short time. If he took more blood, he could loosen the power I laid upon him. Therefore I buried the statuette, buried it deep, and believed that it would never be found."

"But it was," said Sheila. "And this demon took blood."

"So it seems," said Eric. He sat straighter in his chair. "So. It has happened. The demon has been found. He has taken blood and more blood, and found those to whom he can speak.

"What does he say to them?" I asked.

"Be free," said Eric.

"Is that it?" I asked.

"Is that not enough?"

"It doesn't sound very bad," I said dubiously.

"Does it not? Think, Mister Jones, what lies within you. Every impulse, every momentary desire, every passing lust: if these were free of the constraints you place upon them, and if you felt free to follow every thought, where would you go? What evil thing would you not do?"

I did not need to look within myself to know that there were things I kept locked away and would wish no one to see or know. All of us have such thoughts and keep them safely locked behind our eyes.

"Vulang speaks to the worst in us, and bids us to free our darkest dreams. We work to make ourselves good, Mister Jones, Miss Balsam. We lean towards the light, strive to be... and Vulang works against that. Those who submit to him seem unchanged yet they are dangerous to those around them - and of course, themselves."

"Can they be saved?" asked Sheila.

Eric looked sadly at her. "That depends on their actions. Some have been too evil, and saving them is not a kindness. Others, well, they will be left with a darkness on their souls which will trouble them for a very long time."

"My mother…"

"Miss Balsam, I do not know. You told me that she was killed, pronounced dead. If that is the case, then I can offer no hope other than to say I will try to free her from her present distress."

Sheila swallowed. "Then that will be enough. Vulang, this demon, he has spoken with me and I have felt his power - I have managed to fight him, but if he has taken my mother I want her free - even if that is to be free to die peacefully."

Eric bowed his head. "Very well. Then I shall confront this demon."

"We," I said simply.

Eric smiled at me. "We," he replied.

"Mister Eric," said Sheila with sudden decision. "I feel responsible for this. I purchased the unicorn statuette. I brought it home. Mine was the first blood it tasted. I must play my part in this."

"And what part can you play, Miss Balsam?" asked Eric. "The demon has already touched you once. It would be easy for it to touch you again. Indeed, it would probably reach for you first."

"Then I am the decoy. You are sure that you can rebind this demon, Mister Eric?"

"I have done it once before, under worse conditions. Here the demon has not fully broken free, and therefore I have an advantage."

"What are you going to need?" I asked Eric.

Eric broke free of his reverie and became entirely practical. "Mister Jones, you are familiar with the cupboard in the hall in which I keep outdoor wear?"

I thought back to my previous visits to this house, and nodded.

"In there, you will find a large black sports bag. Please go and get it."

I hurried to comply, and walked back into the room to find Eric deep in thought.

"Miss Balsam, if you look over to the front window of this room, you will see a chest of drawers, yes?"

"Yes."

"In the top left drawer you will find candles in a number of different colours. Please bring me two white, two yellow and two red."

Sheila walked quickly to the chest of drawers and started picking up candles. As an afterthought, she also picked up two boxes of matches, and put one in her pocket. Carrying the candles awkwardly, she left the drawer open.

"Mister Jones, please open the bag and tell me what is in there."

I unzipped the bag and took out the few items that were inside.

"Item, two short silver swords." I laid the swords down on the floor beside the bag. "Item, one packet of children's chalks. The yellow is missing... no, it has fallen out. It is broken, partly used." I laid that aside. "Item, leather cords, three of them. Item, a length of silver chain." These things too I laid beside the bag. "Item, length of rope or cord." I put this beside the chain. "Item, half burnt stick of what seems to be dried stuff tied together."

I closed the bag. "That's it."

"There should be something else," said Eric without looking at me.

I felt around in the bag again. "Oh yes, sorry, missed this. It is a small velvet bag." I took it out, and fumbled with the drawstring. "Inside..."

"Please do not open it, Mister Jones."

I looked a little surprised, but laid it down beside the bag, wondering what might be inside.

Eric stood, and picked up each of the items in turn. One by one he laid them on the small table that was positioned below the wall hanging of Vishnu. Then he took the bunch of died herbs from the table behind his chair, lit them in the fire and extinguished the flame. Once again the scent of sage and lavender filled the room. Eric gently wafted the smoke from the herbs across the table where it hung with a strange heaviness over the items placed there.

He turned to us. "I will be gone for a few minutes. Please, take more water if you wish, otherwise wait here for me and do not disturb that table. Mister Jones, we will need transport. Will you please ring for a taxi, to be here as soon as possible?" He left the room.

"What now?" Sheila asked me.

I shrugged. "We wait here. What else is there to do? I'll phone for a taxi."

"Did you believe him, with all that talk about re incarnation and binding of demons?"

"I have seen Eric do some remarkable things, Sheila. I'm going to keep an open mind. And you have spoken with this demon, haven't you? So don't try telling me that wasn't real."

"I know, Mister Jones, it is just that…"

"Here, now, none of it seems real?"

"Yes, that's it. It doesn't feel real."

"Then, Sheila, see how real it feels when we go to your house. You are coming, aren't you?"

"I did say. Just, now I'm having doubts. Mister Jones, I did speak with that… that… that thing. How can this stuff deal with that? I mean, look at it. It's nothing, and He is so strong."

I shrugged again. "Sheila, I can only tell you that I trust Eric."

She frowned, and I realised then how frightened she was of going back to her house.

"Sheila," I said as gently as I could. "Eric does know what he is doing. Trust him. It will all work out."

She did not answer me, and sat in silence until Eric returned. I used the telephone in his hall to call for a taxi whilst I waited. When Eric returned downstairs it was clear that he had showered, and changed his clothes, although the new set of clothing was very similar to the previous set.

"Thank you for waiting," said Eric. "Have you organised the taxi, Mister Jones?"

Even as he asked that, a horn sounded from the road outside. Eric picked up the sports bag, and slowly packed the items from the table into it. The horn sounded again. "Miss Balsam, Mister Jones: perhaps you had better go and keep the driver happy," said Eric quietly.

Sheila went first. At the front door I hung back, watching her walk down the drive. Eric finally joined me at the door. "Eric, is there anything wrong?" I asked him.

"No, nothing for you to worry about, Mister Jones. Just... just this may be the whole point for me of this lifetime, and I am a little nervous. Maybe keyed-up is a better expression?" he added hastily.

I realised that he meant to reassure me with that addition, and for once I patted his arm awkwardly, reassuringly. He flashed me his brilliant smile, his white teeth gleaming in the darkening evening.

"Once more unto the breach!" he declaimed and ushered me out of the house. He closed and locked the door, and led me down the path to the street, where the taxi waited for us. We got into the car, and Eric gave the driver the address.

"OK guv," replied the driver.

The journey passed in silence. I could tell that Eric was becoming increasingly excited, in contrast to Sheila, who sat beside me in the rear of the taxi. She would not look at either me or Eric, but stared bleakly out of the side window of the car. When the driver at last stopped outside her house, she was reluctant to leave the car. I walked around to her door and opened it for her. I offered her my hand, and with a weak smile she took it, and squeezed it hard. I helped her out and closed the door. The taxi drove off leaving us standing there in the road holding hands, and I coloured slightly.

"It would be better if you opened the gate, Miss Balsam," said Eric. I thought his voice was a little over loud, and was slightly put out when he winked at me as she walked past him to the gate.

"Now," said Eric as we all walked slowly towards the front door of the Balsam house. "When we get to the door it is important that Miss Balsam is the one to open the door and then to invite us inside."

Sheila snorted. "That's a silly superstition, surely?"

Eric shrugged. "Silly or not, that is what we will do. Every little helps, Miss Balsam, every little helps. Is there a solid floor in the hall, or is it carpet?"

"Carpet," she replied. "Why?"

"No matter. Have you your keys ready?"

Sheila groped in her bag, and took out her house keys. She waved them. Eric pointed at the door, and she unlocked it, and opened the door wide. The hall was entirely dark now, and I could tell that she was reluctant to enter.

"Sheila, go on!" I hissed, trying to encourage her.

"I can feel him there," she said, and took a step away from the door.

"Miss Balsam! Please!" urged Eric.

Sheila took a deep breath, and screwed up her courage, her face and closed her eyes. She took a step across the threshold of her home, and staggered, losing her balance. She grabbed at the door for support, and her other hand flailed wildly. Her bag hit the statuette of the unicorn, which rocked on its stand.

"Enter," she gasped, and fell to her knees.

Eric leapt across the threshold and falling to his own knees caught the statuette as it overbalanced and fell towards the floor. I hurried into the hall, and went to help Sheila, who had turned very pale.

"I can hear him," she said in a strained voice. "I can hear him. He has someone new there, in the circle. Someone strong and tough: his blood will be enough to set Vulang free. I can hear him. Free to desire!"

Eric replaced the statuette on the stand, and looked with dismay at the scratch on his left hand. "It cut me," he said. "It cut me when I caught it."

"Is that a problem?" I asked, kneeling beside Sheila who was prone on the floor and shaking.

Eric looked at me, despair in his face. "It may be the ruin of us all."

Sheila was now on her hands and knees, coughing. "Free to desire," she said again and I looked at her with concern.

"Can you still perform the Binding?" I asked Eric.

"I can carry out the ritual. Will it hold now? I do not know, Mister Jones, I do not know. And faith and certainty are important aspects of this spell."

"Eric!" gasped Sheila.

"Mister Jones," said Eric in a voice that sent a chill down my spine: "I am afraid."

"Eric!" shouted Sheila, and we both looked at her. She pointed down the hall, and we followed her gaze, in dread of what we would see.

*

Ian Evans struggled to get up onto his knees. He was terrified of the shadowman who towered above him. The exhultation of the three women horrified him, but he was determined to resist whatever was to happen as best he could. The candles flickered and the unnatural flames they created rose higher and higher until they arched above the circle and the celebrants who surrounded it.

The shadowman raised his arms, and looked upwards at the

flames. "I am the great god Vulang," he roared. "After centuries in darkness, as was foretold for me I am again to be free upon this earth, to spread the desire for freedom amongst all! Free To Desire!"

"Free to desire! Free to desire! Free to desire!" chanted Jane, Maria and Mrs Balsam in turn. The echoes ran around the cellar, and Evans turned his head trying to follow them.

"Here in this temple we shall start," said Vulang. "Here we shall begin our work." He looked around at the ornate chairs and the glowing, golden circle. "This shall be the start, yet loosening the ties that bind and freeing your true natures will change this place beyond measure. Marble, gold and gems shall flow here, and many shall come in worship!"

"Power," said Mrs Balsam in a dark and awful voice.

"Power will be yours, power in measure beyond your dreams! The corners of the world at your feet."

"Pain," hissed Maria.

"Pain you shall cause, pain in all its dreadful and most awful forms shall be your feast and your delight."

"Lust," purred Jane.

"Sensual delights beyond imagining await once you set yourself free."

Vulang turned his dark gaze upon Ian, kneeling within the circle. "You see what I offer? Freedom, Freedom from petty constraints, from cheap morality and false gods. Freedom to be yourself, in your most true nature."

His dark will beat down upon Ian, who found himself imagining many, many things. Richly dressed as an emperor, in a mansion on a hilltop, his hands flowing with coin. Everywhere he turned, rich furniture from the four corners of the world lay around him, gems and gold, wealth beyond any dream lay waiting. It was his, all was to be his, he only had to... Evans snatched back his hand, realising that he had been about to clasp hands with the dark one before him.

Vulang smiled at him. "Little soul, I see within you." He looked at Jane, "You have done well, my pet, my angel. So very well. Here indeed is one who can fill the fourth chair that stands empty. She who was here before was not so worthy as this one, for the depth of her desires was shallow."

He started to walk slowly around the glowing circle. As he passed each black candle, the flames bent themselves to him and wrapped themselves around his body, before returning to arc above the circle. Vulang paused beside each chair, and gave each occupant a long, lingering kiss.

"What do you want from me?" gasped Evans.

"Why, nothing will I take from you," replied Vulang, with a smile.

"That I don't believe," Evans managed. "Liar and trickster, you are, no true god."

Vulang roared in anger. The sound echoed and re echoed around the cellar. Maria bared her teeth at Evans in rage. The single lightbulb dangling from the ceiling shattered, and the glass rained down on Evans.

"Puny mortal!" snarled Vulang. "What need of lies have I? I bring freedom, the freedom you all claim to crave so deeply. Lies? Have you looked into your soul, and seen the lies you tell yourself each day? For I can see them as I stand here, Ian Evans!"

He continued his procession around the circle. Evans had to twist around to see the shadowman, but had no wish to leave his back turned upon the monster.

"Aye, monster you think me? Yet I am not. I am honesty, that virtue you praise daily in your petty tasks. I give you the strength and power to be honest with yourself, to be true to your full nature, to live as your maker intended you to live. Not hide away inside a shell made for you by others."

Vulang paused beside Jane. "Look at this one. You enjoyed her last night, did you not? And she enjoyed you?" Jane nodded vigorously. "You pleased each other, where is the harm in that? You both took what you wanted, and had no need to fear the thoughts of others."

Jane looked up, and reached for the shadowman, but he moved from her grasp, and walked again.

"I see into you, Ian Evans. Do you see this chair?" Vulang stopped next to the single empty chair, and he caressed the ornate back. Evans could see now that the carvings were coins, jewels, gems and chests overflowing with golden cups and necklaces. "This is the chair for the one who above all desires wealth. I see into you Ian Evans, and I tell you that you were born for this chair. You wish for wealth, do you not? I see you were born into poverty. I see your parents, dying early, worn out by the struggle to provide for you as poorly paid jobs were given - then taken from them, and granted again - for such a brief space. I see your nightly woes as a child, the times you went to bed hungry for lack of food, the times there were no lights within your house...the times you were cold for the lack of heating...I see the dreams that find you cold and homeless, begging on the streets for your next cheap meal... or for a hot, warming, drink on a chill day. I see how you despise those who stride across this land, with compassion on their lips and hatred for the poor in their hearts and hands."

Evans let out a sob and threw his handcuffed hands over his eyes. Vulang bent towards him, and held out a hand, not quite touching the golden ring.

"I see what drives you now, Ian Evans. It is not compassion for the others around you who suffer as you did, not compassion for those who nightly freeze on the cold streets, but the burning desire never to experience that again. Who would want to?"

Tears of anger and frustration ran down Ian's cheeks.

"Take my hand, Ian Evans. Just take my hand and I can show you how. I can gift you the freedom you crave, which will release you from this dread. Be free, follow your deep desires, and your hands will flow with gold, and you will never again know that despair."

Vulang flicked the fingers of his left hand, the golden circle flared, and Evans felt the handcuffs binding his hands vanish. "I do not Bind," said the demon in lofty tones. "I bring release. All you have to do is reach out to me and the freedom to break your own fetters will be yours."

Evans sobbed again, a wracking sound drawn from deep within him. Without looking up from the floor, his left hand started to reach out, the choice made. The demon began to reach out to take Evans' hand: but stopped. Instead of crouching down, he rose, and spreading his arms wide spun around, seeking the sudden source of his disquiet. "One comes, one I have known before," he hissed. He walked around the circle until he reached Maria's chair, and he bent fondly down towards her. She looked up at the demon with adoration.

"Go, child of my heart," he told her. "Find them, and release your deepest joy upon them."

Maria stood and kissed the demon lingeringly. Then she turned and walked to the steps leading from the cellar, and slowly began to climb.

Vulang gazed at Ian Evans, who still crouched in the circle. "Be still, my child," he said. "The sadness will pass. I shall return in a few moments and we will complete the ritual, and you may join with me and be free of the pain for ever." He walked slowly around the circle, the candles still each wrapping him briefly with their dark flames, until he reached the Master's Chair on which he had been seated. The demon ran his hand lovingly over the ornate carvings, and was gone.

Chapter Thirteen

Eric looked down the length of the hall and gasped. A dark, stocky figure emerged from the doorway to the kitchen, and stood at the end of the hall as if waiting.

"Who is that?" he asked.

"That is my cleaner, Maria," Sheila told him.

"Is she the one who chased you and Mister Jones when you fled to the taxi?"

"Yes," I replied.

"And she is dead?" asked Eric.

"She doesn't look very dead to me," I told him.

"Appearances can be very deceptive," Eric answered. He quickly opened his sports bag, and threw one of the silver swords to me, hilt first.

"What am I meant to do with this?" I asked him, catching the sword awkwardly.

"Stop her from coming down here, whilst I do my work," replied Eric. He pulled his chalk from the sports bag, and started to draw a circle on the floor. "Oh," he added, "and take care. I'm sure that she is dangerous." He pulled Sheila close to him, and began whispering urgently to her.

I eyed Maria, who shifted her stance. Feeling at the same time exposed, unsafe and faintly ridiculous, I brandished the silver sword and walked down the hallway towards her. In the darkness at the end of the hall, the faint gleam from the sword was the only illumination, and I ran my left hand along the wall for both balance and comfort. When I reached the bottom of the stairs, I stopped. I turned to look at Eric, who shouted to me at once:

"Don't take your eyes off her, Mister Jones! And keep the sword between you at all times."

I faced front, as it were, again, and saw that Maria had moved closer to me when I wasn't watching her. I raised the silver sword awkwardly, and pointed the tip at her.

"I am walking up behind you, Mister Jones, don't jump," called Sheila.

I am afraid that I was startled when the first thing to arrive in my peripheral vision was not her hair, but the tip of the other silver sword. Maria recognised Sheila, and snarled in a most unattractive way. Sheila slipped her left arm around my waist for comfort - comfort for which of us, I am not sure. Behind us, I could hear the sound of Eric continuing his preparations. Maria took a step forward, but a little to one side. Both Sheila and I swung the points of our swords to follow her movement. Maria's eyes opened wide, and were glowing with an inner crimson fire. The light splashed onto the silver swords, staining them a blood red: the only brightness in that dark hall.

"I seem to have made a bit of a mistake," called Eric from behind us. Instinctively we both turned to look at him, and Maria leaped at us.

I gasped and swung my sword at her in a wild back-handed sweep, missing her as she dodged. Her demon haunted eyes gave her much better vision in the darkness. Sheila however thrust firmly at Maria, and her sword caught Maria's outstretched arm as she reached for us.

Maria screamed, an unearthly and unsettling, indeed a non human sound. She staggered backwards, her right hand clutching her other arm. I flashed my sword towards her again, and Maria stepped back towards the kitchen door. Sheila pulled away from me, and I stepped into the very centre of the hall.

"You shall not pass," I said under my breath, and giggled stupidly. I could sense Sheila leave my side.

"I must help Eric," she whispered.

Maria spoke then, but in a cultured, male voice that I knew instinctively was not hers.

"He will need more help than you can give, failed child. Run, I counsel you, run."

Behind me I could hear Sheila make a half concealed sob, and Eric started talking to her in an undertone. I swallowed, and took a fresh grip on my sword, raising it to point at Maria's face.

"And you, standing before me, what are you?" was the amused response to my defiance.

"Me?" My voice sounded thin and weak even in my own ears, and the darkness of the true night seemed to grow and fill the end of the hall. Maria's eyes lost their crimson glow, and dulled. But those same demonic eyes reappeared a moment later, and I understood that although I could not see him, I faced the ancient demon himself. I held the silver sword out before me, as threateningly as I could. Maria stepped backwards again, and disappeared into the kitchen. From the empty doorway I could now hear muffled voices, and the sound of a scuffle.

"You. I see into you, and you are such a little person, a little man... Mister Jones. Such a small thing. Yet I can feel your desire to be more than you are, to be strong in every way. Would you like strength? Would you like the strength to take what you wish? I can give it to you. I can see that you greatly desire that. What would you give to me for that strength?"

I swallowed, and with an effort I kept the silver sword pointing at those glowing eyes that hung, it seemed, upon the wall. "What would you want?" I asked, fervently wishing that Eric would hurry up with this Binding.

"Nothing that you cannot spare."

A faint light arose in the kitchen, and came closer. Maria stood in the doorway, holding a candle. Shadows fell across the hall, moved quickly, and in an instant the shadowman stood before me, the horn rising from his noble brow clear and distinct. I swallowed again, and took one step backwards. The demon smiled, sensing victory.

"You know what you want, Mister Jones. I know what you want. I can free you, for that is my gift."

"You... you don't know what I want," I replied. The tip of my sword drooped.

"I do. I do. Come, take my hand and it is yours. Strength is your desire, the strength of purpose you lack. Have you not drifted, alone and forgotten through this life? Who knows your name, Mister Jones? I can sense that in you, the desire not to be one of the forgotten, whose lives pass like the mist, worthless, unnamed and lost. I can give you what you crave."

Behind me I could hear Eric's voice, low and calm, chanting verses and that gave me strength. I raised the sword again. "You can give me nothing, demon."

"I am the great god Vulang." The horn dipped towards me, and the demon's voice became imperious and commanding. "Say my name!"

I tried to speak, but no sound could I make. The horn came closer to my face, the demon's crimson eyes ablaze with triumph. Suddenly, the strength the demon offered was there within me, gifted for but a moment but I responded.

"No!" I shouted, and cut at the shadow horn with the silver sword. The sword passed right through the shadow. My eyes must have been dazzled by the demon's gaze, for it seemed to me for a moment that the sword left a trail of stars as it went.

The demon hissed and withdrew. "You think that you can defy me? Trust me, little Mister Jones, you do not have that strength within you. I *know* that."

"Don't bet on that," I stammered. "Now go." I slashed at the demon with the sword, averting my eyes in fear. The demon drew back, and that gave me confidence. In that moment, Eric made a satisfied noise, and a faint light arose behind me. I was tempted to look at what was happening, but did not dare. Maria raised her candle higher, and then threw it at my head. I screamed as the hot wax splashed across my face, catching my right eye, and blinding my vision. I waved the sword vaguely but the demon was gone, past me in that instant, striding down the hall towards Eric.

Maria's mouth gaped wide, and she leapt at me. But in a last moment of strength, I raised my sword, and she ran straight onto it. I struggled to keep hold of the hilt as she screamed and pulled herself free of the silver blade. Maria staggered backwards into the kitchen, and fell heavily to the floor. I pulled the sword free, and scrabbled frantically at the wax now congealing on my face, clawing the bits away from my skin.

I knew I could not face the demon again, but maybe I could still do something useful, I thought. I stumbled into the kitchen, and fumbled for the light switch, as I could hear muffled voices from behind a cupboard door. Scared of what demon haunted monster might rise, I put my shoulder to the door, and tried not to step onto Maria's body. I looked down and coughed at the smoke rising from the wound made by the silver blade.

Behind me, I heard Eric give a wordless cry, and Sheila scream. I heard the demon shout: "Again we meet - but this time I win!"

*

Ian Evans scrambled to his feet, and looked around the cellar. Vulang had gone, and in his absence the candles surrounding the circle dimmed, and the flames fell back offering a smaller light. Mrs Balsam sank back into her chair, and stared at him impassively. He turned to look at Jane.

"Is that, is that what he offered you?" Evans asked in a halting voice.

Jane looked at him steadily. "We each are offered what we want most," she told him. "I needed love. I am an only child, my parents died when I was young, and I spent time with relatives, foster carers and in homes. I needed..." her eyes dropped.

"Jane, you know that it isn't real, don't you?"

"It's real to me! It's real for me!"

"No," Evans told her. "He's not given you that. He's made you instead into something you don't need to be."

"Don't listen to him, girl," Mrs Balsam called harshly. "He isn't one of us, he doesn't know."

Evans looked at her. "I know you are dead," he said, and turned back to Jane. "You know that too, Jane. She's dead. You saw her body, didn't you? You know she's dead, and that this has to be wrong!"

Jane looked across the circle to where Mrs Balsam sat. "Dead," she repeated. Her expression hardened suddenly. "He is right. You are dead. I saw you, dead in the kitchen!" She stood up out of her chair, the chair carved with ornate images of lust and desire. She suddenly kicked at the chair, and it slid sideways away from her. One leg nearly touched the glowing circle, and Mrs Balsam jerked up out of her chair, the chair of power and subjugation.

"Don't touch the circle!" she shouted, the order filling the cellar with sound and her fury.

Jane looked at her, and raised her arm. She pointed a finger across the circle, and again shouted: "You're dead!"

Evans looked from one to the other, a sudden hope rising. He reached out to Jane, but when his hand crossed the chalk circle, it flared with power, and he snatched his hand away, with a cry of pain. Mrs Balsam laughed. Jane dropped her arm, and Mrs Balsam laughed again. "Yes, you *will* do as I bid!" she cried.

"No." Jane looked to her left. "You are dead. Dead things shouldn't walk. The dead should not have dominion over us." Jane deliberately reached out and toppled the nearest candle. The black candle fell to the floor and went out. The black iron stand fell across the glowing, golden chalk circle, which flared and went out. Jane made an anguished sobbing noise, and fell to the floor. Mrs Balsam cried out, and slumped back into her chair.

Evans looked around. The remaining candles shed some light, just enough to allow him to see around the cellar. He stepped out of the now broken circle, and knelt beside Jane. She turned away from him.

"What have I done?" she sobbed.

"Nothing bad," Evans told her. He tried to take her in his arms, but she shrank away from him.

"You've got nothing on," she said, and looked away.

Evans looked around the cellar. In one corner was a torn sheet, and he wrapped that around his waist, and tied it. "Better?" he asked.

She nodded, without really looking at him.

"Come on," Evans said to her. "We need to get out of here." He looked across the circle. Mrs Balsam lay slumped and still in the chair, the candles flickering on either side of her.

"But he... he..."

"Well, if he comes back here we are lost, aren't we?" said Evans practically. "Let's get out of here." He looked around again. "Unless you'd rather wait for him to come back?"

Jane shook her head. Evans tried to put an arm around her waist, but she pulled away. "Don't touch me, I don't feel clean," she said. But she did allow him to hold her hand, and lead her up the stone steps towards the kitchen.

At the top of the steps, Evans pushed at the door. It moved a little. "There's something stopping it opening, something on the other side." Evans pushed harder, and the door started to open. Light from the kitchen flooded into the space at the top of the cellar steps, and Evans put his shoulder to the door and pushed as hard as he could. He could feel a resistance, as someone - or something - pushed back. The door finally fell open, and he could hear a body fall to the floor with a gasp.

Evans gave a shout and jumped into the kitchen, his fists raised for a fight. But he stopped when he saw Mister Jones who had fallen back against a cabinet, a silver sword on his right hand and a livid, bright red mark across his face. A body lay face down at his feet and Evans stepped across it to offer Mister Jones his hand, and pulled him to his feet.

"Mister Jones! You don't know how glad I am to see you!" Evans said.

"Likewise, Ian," replied Mister Jones.

Jane climbed over Maria's body, and looked down on her with revulsion. "I want to get out of here," she said.

Mister Jones pointed to the back door. "You can get out that way."

Jane ran to the door, and tugged it open. Then she paused, realising that her clothing was at best skimpy. "Where can we go?" she asked Evans.

"Go next door," replied Mister Jones. "That's my house, you'll find something there you can put on."

"I'll follow you in a moment," called Ian Evans as Jane ran out into the dark garden without another word.

Evans looked at Jones' damaged face. "Was that the demon?" he asked.

Mister Jones shook his head wearily, and pointed at the body with his sword. "She had a candle. Threw it at me."

"So, where is the demon? Has it fled?" asked Evans.

"No," replied Mister Jones. "It went that way." He pointed to the hall. "Come on."

Evans looked at him reluctantly. Mister Jones walked into the hall, and Evans followed him. They looked down the length of the hall towards the front door. Eric knelt within a circle, lit by six candles arranged outside the ring in an alternating sequence of colours. Before him lay a black cord, with three large knots tied in it. A silver pentacle hung around his neck, glowing bright in the candle light. Also in front of him stood a small copy of the statuette of the unicorn, and in his hands was the length of silver chain. Sheila Balsam stood outside of the circle with the other sword held firmly in both hands. She was in front of the large terracotta statuette of the unicorn.

Before them both towered the shadowman, the demon Vulang, intent on breaking the remaining power that bound him to the statuette and gaining his freedom.

"I bind you, demon..." intoned Eric.

"Your binding, will not prevail, little man," shouted Vulang. "I heard you before, you have made a mistake!"

"I Bind you now because it is your hour.

I Bind you now because it is my power.

I Bind you now because it is MY HOUR!"

"I will smash that which was my prison!" Vulang hissed, and stepped towards the statuette.

Sheila swallowed hard, but kept the silver sword raised firmly at the demon, protecting the terracotta prison.

"You are a failed child!" cried Vulang. "You cannot defy me!"

Sheila swallowed again, but stood her ground. The demon raised his arm and struck at her. But she tilted the sword protectively, and Vulang drew back, unwilling to risk contact with the weapon.

"I Bind you now because it is your hour.

I Bind you now because it is my power.

I Bind you now because it is MY HOUR!"

repeated Eric. He placed one end of the silver chain across the small unicorn, and Vulang screamed. The demon lunged at Sheila, but again she swung the sword at him, and hissing he recoiled.

"Constringo! Constringo! Constringo!" shouted Eric, and wrapped the silver chain entirely around the model. Then he collapsed and lay still.

No one moved as we all gazed at the tall, threatening demon with the commanding horn rising from his brow.

"Failed!" exhulted Vulang. "Failed! Now, I am free!" He flung his head back and laughed, wildly, arrogantly. Evans and Mister Jones flinched at the sound, but Sheila Balsam stood her ground determinedly. Eric twitched, and Sheila inclined her head as if to listen to him.

"He has nothing to say to you, failed child," crowed the demon. "Stand aside!" Vulang stepped imperiously towards Sheila, and obediently she lowered her sword, and stepped aside. Ian Evans let out a groan of despair, and the demon shouted triumphantly. He reached out to the statuette to shatter it forever - and Sheila's right foot deliberately scuffed Eric's chalked circle, breaking it.

From nowhere, a wind arose, howling down the length of the corridor towards the front door. Sheila staggered in the blast, but the demon was buffeted and thrown into the air. The terracotta unicorn opened its mouth and Vulang screamed then, a long unrelenting scream of pain, misery and dread. His arms reached out for Sheila, but she ducked, and with a last lingering, despairing wail the shadowman was drawn irresistibly within the unicorn statuette.

Evans cried out as he was knocked down from behind. First Maria's body whirled down the hallway, turning to mist and following Vulang into the statuette: then last of all Mrs Balsam herself staggered into the hall. Her eyes were dark and blank, and she looked at no one present as the magewind seized her, turned her to a black smoke and flung her into the dark abyss. Soundlessly the unicorn's mouth closed, and the wind stilled.

Mister Jones looked down the length of the hall to where Sheila stood upright, her hair blown around her and the silver sword still raised, now in triumph. "I thought Eric and the demon said he had made a mistake, that he had failed?" he asked. "What happened?"

"Oh, said Sheila, lowering her blade, "the mistake was nothing. He was inside his circle of power, and the candles needed to be lit. They were outside, but I had matches in my pocket. That was Eric's plan, to make the demon think he could win."

"I thought he had, when nothing happened!" said Mister Jones, walking down the hall towards Sheila. "I can't believe how brave you were!"

Eric groaned from the floor, and Sheila smiled down at him. "Eric told me the demon would get past you, and to let the demon get as close as I dared, and then to break the circle. He wanted the demon as close as possible before releasing the

Binding Spell by breaking the circle that contained it."

"You could have told me!" Mister Jones said. "I was frightened for you!"

Sheila Balsam laughed, and looked at the terracotta statuette. "Vulang got me completely wrong, Mister Jones. He thought I wanted money most of all, and tempted me with that. He failed because although I do want not to be poor, most of all I wanted the courage to stand up for myself. He gave me that too - and it was his undoing."

"What will you do with it now?" Mister Jones asked.

Eric sat up on the floor, amidst the ruins of his circle of power and the tools he had needed to remake the Binding. "The desert?" he suggested.

Sheila Balsam looked at the two men, and at Ian Evans who was still beside the kitchen door. "I'll package it up, and it can go in my loft. No, better yet: the package can go in my cellar which I'll have blocked up. I shan't want to use it again, and he will feel at home there with Maria and my mother for company."

"Isn't that a bit cruel?" asked Mister Jones.

Sheila Balsam gave him a steely look. "It's no more than he deserves."

About the author

Will Macmillan Jones lives in Wales, a lovely green, verdant land with a rich cultural heritage. He does his best to support this heritage by drinking the local beer and shouting loud encouragement whenever International Rugby is on the TV. A fifty something lover of blues, rock and jazz he has just fulfilled a lifetime ambition by filling an entire wall of his home office with (full) bookcases. When not writing, he is usually lost with the help of a satnav on top of a large hill in the middle of nowhere.

His major comic fantasy series, released by Red Kite Publishing, can be found at:

www.thebannedunderground.com

and information on his other work and stuff in general at :

www.willmacmillanjones.com

There's a blog. There's always a blog, isn't there?

www.willmacmillanjones.wordpress.com

Made in the USA
Charleston, SC
19 March 2016